Missouri:
Faith Came Late

This Large Print Book carries the Seal of Approval of N.A.V.H.

Missouri:
Faith Came Late

Variety Is the Spice of Romance
in the Show-Me State

Freda Chrisman

Thorndike Press • Waterville, Maine

Copyright © 1997 Barbour Publishing, Inc.

Missouri #3

Scripture quotations are taken from the King James Version of the Bible.

Published in 2006 by arrangement with
Barbour Publishing, Inc.

Thorndike Press® Large Print Christian Fiction.

The tree indicium is a trademark of Thorndike Press.

The text of this Large Print edition is unabridged.
Other aspects of the book may vary from the original edition.

Set in 16 pt. Plantin by Al Chase.

Printed in the United States on permanent paper.

Library of Congress Cataloging-in-Publication Data

Chrisman, Freda.
    Faith came late : variety is the spice of romance in the
show-me state / by Freda Chrisman.
        p. cm. — (Missouri ; #3) (Thorndike Press large print
Christian fiction)
    ISBN 0-7862-8425-0 (lg. print : hc : alk. paper)
    1. Women school principals — Fiction.   2. Clergy —
Fiction.   3. Missouri — Fiction.   4. Large type books.
I. Title.   II. Series.   III. Thorndike Press large print
Christian fiction series.
PS3603.H73F35 2006
    813´.6—dc22   2005036365

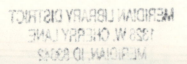

Dedicated to the memory
of our precious grandson

Josiah Daniel Chrisman
1981–1989

As the Founder/CEO of NAVH, the only national health agency solely devoted to those who, although not totally blind, have an eye disease which could lead to serious visual impairment, I am pleased to recognize Thorndike Press* as one of the leading publishers in the large print field.

Founded in 1954 in San Francisco to prepare large print textbooks for partially seeing children, NAVH became the pioneer and standard setting agency in the preparation of large type.

Today, those publishers who meet our standards carry the prestigious "Seal of Approval" indicating high quality large print. We are delighted that Thorndike Press is one of the publishers whose titles meet these standards. We are also pleased to recognize the significant contribution Thorndike Press is making in this important and growing field.

Lorraine H. Marchi, L.H.D.
Founder/CEO
NAVH

* Thorndike Press encompasses the following imprints: Thorndike, Wheeler, Walker and Large Print Press.

Chapter 1

"You . . . you menace!" she shouted. "Are you blind?"

Ignoring other Kansas City shoppers, Julie Richmond bent down to collect her parcels strewn on the street.

"No, miss," he said, "I have good vision. Now if —"

"I have news for you, *mister;* you need glasses!"

"Miss, if you'll calm down and let me drive my car to the curb, I'll help you," he pleaded.

"Go on! You've done enough for me."

Uttering a disgruntled objection, the man retrieved a sack lying just under his silver sports car.

"Please, miss, we're blocking traffic. Let me —"

"*You're* blocking traffic! I am trying to recoup after almost being knocked down by a crazy driver!"

"I beg your pardon, miss. You shouldn't have stepped off the curb without checking to your left. The light changed; I had the right-of-way," he reasoned.

Anger consumed Julie's fatigue. *Another*

self-righteous male! She dropped the last package into her shopping bag, got to her feet, and her eyes traveled way up to look at the man in front of her. He was not only a menace, he was gargantuan! Unusually tan for the month of May, he had black hair and penetrating brown eyes.

"Well," she spat, "what are you waiting for? Get in your car and stop blocking traffic!"

"I can't leave until I'm sure you're all right."

"Of course I'm 'all right.' Can't you see?"

The man gave her a slow grin. "You look great to me."

Julie's face burned. Clustering around them, a small crowd listened to their heated conversation. Some even chuckled at his remark. He added a final affront.

"May I take you wherever you're going? You may be more shaken up than you realize."

Julie took charge. "No, thank you! I'm perfectly capable of deciding if I need help, and I don't. Move your car, and the sideshow will be over."

She lifted her chin, saw the light was in her favor, and crossed the street with what dignity he had left her.

Her shopping done, Julie reached home

an hour later. She heard them as soon as she got out of her car. What now? The house was well-constructed, like most of those built back in the thirties, but no house could completely muffle Sid and Ethel Richmond's arguments. Mentally turning off her parents' enraged voices, she went inside.

Never, never would it happen to her, she vowed, as she slipped up the stairs. Marriage was a joke as far as Julie was concerned. Her parents hadn't celebrated a single day of nonaggression in her memory. And they weren't the only ones. Most couples she knew had lousy relationships. They traded dirty slurs, cut each other down in public, cheated on their marriage, or all of the above.

In her room, Julie threw her carryall on the bed. Then, tossing back her long hair, she hung up her jacket.

"Hi, Julie. Did you just get home?"

It was Colleen, the baby of the family. She was graduating from Kinner High this month.

"Yeah, honey, and I have something for you."

Julie pulled a parchment sack from the carryall and, out of it, a pink velvet box. Glass shattered against the wall in the next room, and Colleen's eyes filled with tears.

Julie frowned. Colleen usually got home about four o'clock. No doubt she'd heard the whole malignant session from the beginning.

"Forget them, Colleen. Close your mind. That's what I do. Here," Julie said, handing her the box. "This will make you feel better."

Colleen's gift was an opal pendant in a gold filigree setting. They'd seen it in the window of Vontell's Jewelry, and Julie promised it to Colleen if she made valedictorian.

"Oh, Julie," her sister gasped as she opened the box, "it's the prettiest thing I've ever owned. Thank you!" She started to hug Julie, but raucous sounds erupted again, and Colleen's face clouded. "I wish they wouldn't ruin every evening, especially this one."

"Speak for yourself, kiddo. My evening's fine. I don't let them get to me the way you do. Neither does Lisa."

"Oh, Lisa! She's never home long enough to let them bother her. If she's not out with her boss, she's dating Curt when he's in town." Colleen sighed. "Curt's through with his tests at Washington U. He'll be home anytime."

Julie noticed Colleen's softened voice.

"That's another thing that shouldn't worry you. Curtis Graham is Lisa's emergency kit, a fill-in when no one else is available."

"I'm not so sure about that. Curt's been home a lot lately. You remember his sister, Rosemary? She works in TWA reservations and gets a discount for him."

"Lucky guy!"

Julie regretted her offhand remark. The reason Curt came home so often was to see Lisa. But Colleen was deep in her thoughts.

"Rosemary says this was a hard year for Curt. I don't think the Grahams approve of all his dates with Lisa. They think he should study more when he's home. It's not his fault, though. She's the one who insists on going out. He'll be a great doctor if she'll stop getting in his way."

"Has it occurred to you that letting Lisa interrupt his study schedule speaks badly for his commitment to medicine?" Julie asked. "If he didn't fly home so often, he'd have more time to study."

Colleen looked away. "I don't mean to hurt your feelings, Julie, but you don't give any man the benefit of the doubt."

"I'm not hurt, and you're right. I've never met a man I felt I could really trust. Added to that, they're reckless, discourteous, and uninteresting."

Colleen's face flushed. "Maybe if you weren't assistant principal of a girls school . . ."

"Don't be embarrassed, honey. I understand what you're saying." She broke into a sing-song lilt. "You think my selection of men is limited by my job and that I'm a prejudiced woman who wouldn't recognize an interesting man if I saw one."

"I don't think that, Julie," Colleen returned softly.

Now she'd hurt her feelings. Julie hadn't meant to sound so cynical. Taking the pink box from Colleen's hand, she shared her latest frustration.

"I did meet a man. Today. He almost killed me with his car, the big oaf. He met the exact criteria I mentioned before."

Oddly, Colleen's face brightened as Julie's bleak criticism went on.

"I was crossing the street, going back to my car. When I stepped off the curb, out of nowhere came this *mutant* in his silly-looking sports car." Colleen was still smiling, but Julie was done. "Now turn around, and I'll put your necklace on you. Since the free-for-all next door has run out, let's enjoy a moment of peace. Are you excited about graduation?"

A smile lingered on Colleen's face, and

12

Julie wondered why she was intimidated by it.

Withering glares and bitter jibes charged the air between Sid and Ethel at dinner. Unnoticed by either of them, Colleen's hands shook as she ate. Their parents, day by day, gnawed at Colleen's self-esteem in spite of Julie's efforts to thwart them. Julie wished Lisa were there now. She always missed the choice battles. But there was a reason she did: She planned her days to avoid them.

When Sid was home from his territory, Lisa ate out with Leonard Sherry, her boss. Then they went back to work late at the office. He was the senior partner of Sherry and Winwood, Attorneys at Law. By the time she got home that evening, dinner would be over, the Richmonds would have quarreled themselves out, and Lisa wouldn't be expected at work until noon tomorrow.

"I see Lisa's taking dinner with the old man again," Sid Richmond observed, chewing as he talked.

Ethel shot him a frigid glance. "It's obvious, isn't it? She's not here. And why shouldn't she go out to dinner with Mr. Sherry? She'll have a steak."

If you'd called me, we could be eating

steak, too, Mother, thought Julie. No matter, dinner would have been just as bad. Her mother was not a good cook. She didn't even like to cook. Julie wondered how Ethel could prepare meals for nearly thirty years and still put together a dinner as tasteless as the one they were eating. Everything was overcooked, except the meat loaf. It was a culinary disaster.

Julie searched for a safe subject. "How did your sales meeting go today, Dad?"

Ethel snorted, and Colleen ducked her head to fork a piece of limp broccoli.

"Oh, those idiots came up with an agenda straight out of a comic book. If they'd let me handle those meetings, I'd show those college boys the *right* way to sell feed supplements."

"Go ahead, genius, tell us some of your big ideas," Ethel challenged with a smirk.

"Mother, please," started Colleen.

Julie rescued her. "Let's not quarrel, folks. The family's together, except for Lisa, of course. But we should make it a pleasant time. You know what the dietitians say: Food digests better in a calm atmosphere."

Ethel sighed and rolled her eyes. "Not another lecture from the professor, I hope."

"No, Mother, I'm trying to promote a quiet conversation," she explained, maneuvering her potatoes away from the grease oozing out of her meat loaf. "We've all been busy today, and it's time to relax."

Colleen looked at Julie and smiled, but neither Sid nor Ethel was ready to call a truce. The malicious contest continued until dishes of lumpy pudding unmercifully ended the meal.

Julie heard Colleen's door close. She put on an emerald satin robe over her gown and swept down the hall, brushing her hair dry. As she suspected, Colleen was stretched out across her bed, crying.

"Honey, honey, don't let them upset you," Julie cooed, dropping her brush to pull Colleen into her arms.

Clinging to her, Colleen sobbed, "It wasn't another quarrel. Curt came by to see Lisa. He just got in town. Julie, he hardly looked at me." Another shudder of tears.

"Honey, there must be guys at Kinner as good-looking and interesting as Curtis Graham," Julie consoled, stroking her sister's back.

"Not to me. Don't talk like I'm a baby, Julie. You know Curt's the only one I'll ever love."

Julie leaned back and eyed her sister. "How did the two of us ever wind up in the

15

same family? You can think of nothing better than having a man in love with you, and I can think of nothing worse. An evening out to dinner and a concert or the theater is nice, but give me mine with a stalwart soul who bids me good night and *leaves!*"

"But you're twenty-seven," Colleen lamented. "Don't you ever let a man you go out with kiss you good night?"

"Sometimes I can't avoid it. After that, I'm busy the next time he calls."

"But you'll never get married if you keep that up," Colleen whimpered, and she cuddled in Julie's arms again. "You'll be an old maid."

"Bingo! I think you've got the picture. This lady will die happy, with her books and her travels and the best clothes she can put in her closet. Not everyone has to have a man to be happy!"

By bedtime, Julie had pumped up Colleen's spirits to the stage of all-out laughter. She'd done it before — lots. She could usually promote a cheerful atmosphere for everyone except her parents. They were impossible.

In her youth, she had wondered why the couple ever married. Now, she ignored the savagery and tried to create a healthier climate for Lisa and, especially, for Colleen. It was what kept her living at home. Because of her mother's frequent swings into irrationality and her father's chronic absence from duty, Julie was the backbone of the family.

Good old dependable Julie. She'd overheard that description of herself last week. Twenty-seven wasn't old, was it? And she was in good shape; she worked out at the school gym every day. She looked at her picture; the yearbook committee had presented one to each faculty member. Actually, it wasn't too bad.

Her skin looked healthy. Her hazel eyes were clear, although she thought their dark lashes and brows made them look too large. Still, her heavy chestnut hair was an asset, her nose wasn't bad, and her lips were not thin like an old maid's were supposed to be.

What the picture didn't show was her height. She was five-foot-seven. Not petite or beautiful like Lisa, she looked to a wide-open future based on intelligence and determination.

Five years before, Julie had taken her master's at Missouri University in Columbia. Breaking away had not been easy. The Richmonds objected only because they wanted her home, bringing in another paycheck. They'd miss her rent money. To Julie, a master's degree was essential, so she stood her ground.

At M.U. she held down an office job and studied harder than she ever had in her life. She made friends, loved the school, and regretted having to come home. Yet, in her two years at Pennington — "A Private School for Young Ladies," the brochures said — she'd grown to love her job as vice-principal.

Julie sat on the bed she had turned back and stacked pillows behind her. She opened her briefcase and, with reading glasses in place, spread a stack of student evaluations on the bed.

Amelia Stewart — she was the first problem. Her teachers had given up on her. In the office she'd heard Miss Clay, her current instructor, commiserating with the teacher Amelia would have in the fall. It was not a happy conversation, hence the evaluation by Julie.

She opened the folder. Amelia Stewart was eight, and she came from a single-parent home. In those cases the source of trouble was sometimes apparent. But Amelia was a minister's daughter. Julie frowned. Well, no one was exempt when a child had problems. He might even be part of it.

A soft tap drew her attention to the door,

and Lisa stepped inside. Her sister's navy blue suit emphasized a shapely figure and the sparkling blue of her eyes.

"Still working your fingers to the bone for the little monsters, I see. Must be a martyr complex."

"No, not at all. It's a pleasure." Julie placed Amelia's folder on top of the others, stacked them aside, and took off her glasses. "How did your evening go?"

Lisa glanced quickly at her. Satisfied the remark was not sarcasm, she sat on the end of the bed and slipped out of her pumps.

"We're getting together the last of a brief. It's always a race to the finish. Leonard goes to court on Monday." She ran her fingers through coppery hair. "How was it here? Did they take a night off?"

"Afraid not. Colleen was upset as usual. I picked up her necklace at the jewelry store. It turned out to be a good evening to give it to her."

"Did she like it?"

"She loved it," answered Julie.

Lisa leaned back on an elbow. "I suppose I'd better find something to give her. I haven't had time to think about it."

Julie wondered if Lisa planned to give Colleen anything at all; she'd only had eighteen years to think about it. But she gave her the benefit of the doubt. *You see, Colleen, I can do it when it makes sense,* she thought.

"Colleen needs to know she's loved, Lisa. A nice gift from you would help."

"You're right. She doesn't get much attention from the folks. What do they think about the scholarship to Lindenwood?"

"I haven't been in on the results. I've only heard the arguments, at full volume. When they ask her about it, Colleens swears she won't know until commencement night."

"Is it true?"

"No, the deed is done; Mom and Dad simply have to accept it," Julie replied. "Colleen's trying to hold off the explosion while Mother tries to persuade *her* she's not capable of living apart from the family. It's a replay of my university days and just as twisted."

"I suppose she probably will leave. But I don't think she'll make it out in the big cruel world either." Lisa lay back and stretched her arms above her head. "You wait and see; she'll be back before Christmas. I can get her a job at the office right now. She'll start as a typist, and they'll let her come back when she drops out of school."

"Oh, Lisa, don't even mention that to her. She already has a summer job at the branch library. Remember? She won't make as much as she would at your office, but she got the job on her own; and it's enough to buy some nice clothes to take with her. By fall I hope she'll look forward to leaving. I've already got her luggage. I plan to give it to her at the last minute to build her confidence."

Lisa jumped to her feet, her eyes blazing with anger.

"I knew you'd do something like that — give her an expensive gift she'd be embarrassed not to use! And you'll make sure she stays there, won't you? Lindenwood is only a short commute from Curt's school. Don't you think I know she's crazy about him? Well, she can't have him; he's mine!"

Julie stood up, too. "I thought you liked older men — Leonard Sherry, for instance."

"I may end up with Len, but until I make up my mind, Curt is my property."

"Lisa, you can't own or manipulate people to suit yourself. You'll break Colleen's heart, and, if Mr. Sherry does propose, you'll throw Curt away."

Lisa's face flushed. "I have a right to make up my own mind!" A frown creased her forehead. "Be honest, Julie. Do you think a popular, handsome guy like Curt Graham could ever fall for a *chunk* like Colleen?"

"Surely you don't look down on her because of a few pounds?"

Lisa picked up her shoes and smiled into the mirror on Julie's dresser.

"I'm realistic," she said.

"Then be realistic enough to have some feeling for her. You're the fashion expert. Forget the competition and give her some tips on her appearance before she goes to school."

"A compliment! I'm thrilled! The god of us all has condescended to let someone else help her manage the family."

"That's a hateful thing to say. I don't manage the family; I try to keep a little harmony going. Stop thinking of yourself, Lisa, and help me."

Giving Julie an icy stare, Lisa crossed the room, yanked open the door, and slammed it behind her.

Chapter 2

Ethel was in a temper because Sid wasn't in town for Colleen's commencement. Appeasing her was impossible, so Julie retreated to her room to dress. Choosing an amber lightweight suit, she piled her hair on top of her head and added green earrings the shade of her eyes. Then, bracing herself, she returned to check on her mother's progress.

At the mirror, Ethel clutched and yanked at her shapeless attire. "I should stay at home!" she declared. Then, with unique logic, she added, "If her own father doesn't care enough to attend Colleen's graduation, why should I? I'll be the only one going alone."

"You'll hardly be alone, Mother. Lisa and I are taking you."

"It's not your responsibility to take me. Sid's supposed to take me. He's never around when I need him. I have to do it *all*."

Lisa appeared in the doorway. "I'm ready to go. I wore this outfit to the office today, but it still looks fresh; and it's almost new," she said, smoothing the sapphire pleats of her skirt with an approving look.

Glad Lisa was on time, Julie picked up her purse to leave. She was ready for a change of scenery. Her mother's clothes were shabby, but there was nothing Julie could do. She had offered to buy her a new dress, but Ethel refused. She'd wait until something more important than a high school graduation came along, she said. Julie hoped Colleen wasn't embarrassed. It was such a special night for her.

"Well, I'm ready. Come on! Let's get through this stupid kiddie exercise," Ethel ordered.

Sharing a look of resignation, Julie and Lisa followed their mother's heavy-footed exit from the house.

Traffic was snarled around the high school, but Julie found a parking space not far from the auditorium. Even though they were early — Julie had seen to that — seats close to the stage were taken.

"Lisa, these seats are terrible," Ethel complained as soon as they sat down. "Go find some better ones. I doubt if they're all gone."

"I'm sure they are, but I'll check."

Julie knew Lisa didn't mind the attention she would get strolling down the aisle, even though, clearly, there were no empty seats.

She was back in seconds, unsuccessful in her search but followed by Curtis Graham. Lisa gave Julie a smug look.

"Look who I found! Some of his friends talked Curt into coming, but he looked so bored I asked him to come back and sit with us. Here, Curt." Lisa patted the chair next to hers. "There's an extra seat right here."

Julie heard: *Here, Prince! Sit!*

Curt spoke to Julie and her mother. Then his fascinated gaze locked on Lisa again.

On stage, faculty and guest speakers filed in as the band struck up the processional. Their eyes straight ahead, Colleen and her classmates marched down the center aisle. With two other students she mounted steps to the stage and now sat facing them. Lisa and Curt were whispering together, ignoring the program. Julie held her breath and hoped Colleen wouldn't look in their direction.

The crowd quieted, and Principal Dayton announced the invocation by Reverend Alex Stewart. Julie's eyes shifted from Colleen to the tall man approaching the podium.

Reverend Alex Stewart? It was the man who had nearly run her down! Could he possibly be? No! He couldn't be Amelia Stewart's father! Nevertheless, Amelia's father *was* a minister.

Julie thought about the conference she had asked the secretary to schedule with him. Amelia's evaluation made it necessary; she'd probably need summer tutoring. But her request was made before their downtown confrontation on the street.

Remorse enveloped her. Never should she have allowed herself to get caught in such a position. She'd lost her temper and made a fool of herself before the parent of one of her students. Now, here in the auditorium, waiting for Colleen's valedictory speech, the episode seemed foolish. Julie gripped her hands and bowed her head as the *Reverend* requested, but she was hardly ready for prayer.

To her relief the tall man sat back down, and she focused full attention on the speaker. Seconds later she gave Alex Stewart a quick glance. He had zeroed in on their row and on her in particular. The slow grin she remembered was there again, and Julie felt her face burn. Lisa noticed her discomfort and jabbed her in the ribs.

"What's wrong with you?"

"Nothing!" Julie shot back.

"We'll talk later."

Irritated again, Ethel hissed, "Be quiet!"

Lisa paid no attention. "Later, I said."

Julie nodded and looked at her program.

Colleen's speech followed ten minutes later, and Julie was in control again. She'd worry about Alex Stewart another time.

Colleen was nervous, yet she presented her speech well; and Julie was proud of her. Her rapt attention to the speaker was bound to signal the obvious for the minister, but Julie didn't care. How could she hold back smiles and applause when she was so proud of Colleen?

Following the ceremony Julie had no problem making a fast getaway. Ethel wasn't interested in socializing. Curt hurried Lisa out, so Colleen had little chance to see them together. She was invited, with other seniors, to celebrate the awards and scholarships they were presented. Since he'd come to the school, Principal Dayton and his wife entertained these groups annually.

So focused was Julie on getting her mother through the crowd, she glanced sideways at Ethel a second too long and ran full tilt into Alex Stewart. Overcome with frustration and embarrassment, she sat down hard.

"Ughh! Ah . . . excuse me," she muttered, not looking at him.

Her purse opened as she fell, and he bent down to help her retrieve its contents.

Ethel, scolding, hovered in the background as people asked Julie if she was hurt. She was conscious of only one speaker.

"We've got to stop meeting like this," Alex Stewart said under his breath.

The silly remark brought Julie to her senses. How dare he be so cavalier! Duty or no duty, she had a consuming desire to forget school procedure and cancel the scheduled conference on the spot.

Dropping the lipstick and comb he handed her into her purse, she ignored his outstretched hand to help her rise, though she chided herself for wearing such a narrow skirt.

Once on her feet she reached for Ethel's arm.

"Let's go, Mother," she said, without glancing at Alex.

Julie heard a soft chuckle as she turned away.

Alex Stewart's eyes followed Julie until she disappeared into the crowd. It was the first time he'd even noticed a girl since Christi's death. Was God trying to tell him something by letting him meet her again?

When she stepped in front of his car that day, he thought he had injured her, and his heart almost stopped. Later, learning she was all right, he was euphoric with the possibility of getting to know her. In her anger she hardly tolerated him.

But, the next day, he took Amelia to school and saw the same girl get out of her car and rush up the steps at Pennington.

"Amelia," he asked as she snapped her tiny plastic purse, "who is that lady?"

The child stopped her move toward a good-bye kiss. "That's Miss Richmond, Daddy. Isn't she beautiful? I wish she was my mommy. You could marry her, you know. I really love her, and I pray for her every night."

He was taken aback and didn't answer right away. "You have to be patient and wait for things to happen, Amelia. God might not think she's the right person for me to marry."

She crossed her ankles, clasped her hands in her lap, and stared straight ahead.

"I guess you're too busy to get a mother for me, aren't you?" she asked with a frown.

"No, it isn't that I'm too busy. God hasn't sent anyone yet," he replied, wondering what she was thinking.

"Sometimes you have to make things happen. You just haven't learned how to do it."

Alex laughed, but Amelia's voice had a

hardness that made him uncomfortable for a moment. Feeling ridiculous, he dismissed the thought.

Tonight at the auditorium they had *collided* again. He'd found out her first name was Julie from the secretary who called about an appointment. He would be busy that day and was thinking of canceling. But now that he'd had a better look, he was eager for their little conference. He'd enjoy hearing how terrific his daughter was from Miss Julie Richmond.

Colleen's usually dull, golden eyes shone as she burst into Julie's room after the party.

"Oh, Julie, we had the best time! Mr. and Mrs. Dayton live in a lovely home, and they're so happy. They say 'dear' and 'sweetheart' when they talk to each other, and they touch hands and smile all the time. It was like heaven. I didn't know a couple could be as happy as they are."

Julie's heart tightened at the poignant longing in Colleen's voice. Decorations and refreshments were secondary. It was the tranquil marriage that impressed her.

"I was proud of you tonight. I knew you were nervous, but you carried off your speech like a pro."

"How did Mother take the presentation

of my scholarship?"

Sitting on the bed, Julie laughed softly. "She choked and swallowed hard for a few minutes, but she pulled through just enough to complain about Dad all the way home."

"And you had to listen." Colleen kissed her sister's forehead. "Poor Julie."

She didn't include Lisa. Julie hoped Colleen's leaving would be the key to a new life for her. Tonight, though she'd probably seen Lisa with Curt, it had taken a routine circumstance — the example of a happy home — to charge her sister with excitement and joy.

Colleen and her mother were both in bed when Lisa got home. In the kitchen, Julie was warming a mug of milk to help her sleep and forget a tension-filled day and night. When Lisa didn't speak, Julie glanced up at her. Lisa's lovely face was void of color.

"What's wrong?" said Julie as she put down her cup. "You look like you've seen a ghost."

"I wish I had. I could handle that."

Julie pulled out a high stool at the breakfast bar. "Come and sit down before you fall down."

The dark blue of her eyes riveting, Lisa

turned to Julie, who perched on a stool beside her.

"A while ago," Lisa said with difficulty, "I saw Dad with another woman."

"Lisa —"

"It's true. Curt saw them, too. They were getting into his car, and, believe me, it's not a mistake. They were together, laughing and enjoying themselves." Tears dropped from her eyes.

Julie felt a suffocating closeness. "But if you saw them for only a moment, you can't be sure."

"We followed them. They went to an apartment house on the south side, and they went in."

"Oh, Lisa." Julie slipped off the stool and wrapped Lisa's trembling body in her arms.

Dad would pull something like this, thought Julie. *It's not enough that our lives are complicated already.* She was furious, too furious to cry.

Lisa reached for a paper napkin to wipe her tears. "I know he's not much," she said, "but he's my father, and I can't hate him. I'm confused. I don't know what to do or say."

Julie's eyes were dry.

"What are we going to do?" Lisa asked.

"Nothing. We're going to let this ride until

we know more. Mother and Colleen couldn't take it. I need to think about it and decide what our options are."

Lisa pulled away. "So, once again, it's Julie to the rescue! I find out about it, and *you're* going to handle it." Lisa crushed the napkin into a ball.

"All right, *you* handle it! *You* take the responsibility. What are you going to do first?"

Julie could see Lisa shrinking into herself. It was a situation she knew only as a lawyer's secretary, not as a personal problem.

"I don't know." Tears shone in Lisa's eyes again. "I'm sorry I said that, Julie. The legal side of separation and divorce is where I dabble." She gripped Julie's arm. "What if he's on his way out? What if he deserts Mother?"

"I suppose we'll cross that bridge when we come to it." Julie pressed her fingertips to her temples. "For now, let's get to bed before someone overhears us."

"How can you think of sleep at a time like this?" Lisa grumbled.

"I doubt I'll sleep any more than you will. The point is, we both need to calm down and see if any ideas come to mind."

Julie sounded a lot more optimistic than she felt.

Neither Julie nor Lisa slept. Julie noticed Lisa's swollen eyes and hoped hers didn't look worse.

Ethel served her usual inedible breakfast of greasy eggs and bacon, and both girls made a show of eating. At Julie's school there would be coffee and rolls for the staff, and she could disappear to work on the summer schedule. Lisa would do even better. Len Sherry, her boss, would order food sent in if Lisa even hinted she was hungry.

"How do you feel this morning, Mother?" Julie inquired and got a *Must you ask?* look from Lisa.

Ethel proceeded to tell all. "Miserable. Absolutely miserable. What with your father out of town, and worrying about Lisa getting in, I didn't sleep a wink." She would have continued, but Lisa cut her off.

"Maybe you can rest today," she suggested, glancing at Julie. "Is Dad coming in early?"

Ethel's laugh was sardonic. "Who can tell? If he happens to call, I'll know then. Otherwise, I'll expect the dear boy when I see him."

Ignoring the sarcasm, Julie asked, "After you've rested, Mother, why don't you make something special to welcome him home? Maybe you could make shortcake for strawberries. That's Dad's favorite dessert, and the berries are so nice this year. Colleen said they had a strawberry torte at the Daytons' last night."

"So that's what they served at their la-di-da party? Well, I'm not impressed. And I don't feel well enough to baby your father," said Ethel.

Julie tried again. "If you should decide on the shortcake after you rest, call me, and I'll bring the berries and whipping cream. Lisa, you'll be home for dinner, won't you?" she said, a slight threat in her voice.

Lisa obviously got the point. "Yes, I'll be here," she answered without enthusiasm.

"One of you go to the stairs and yell at Colleen," ordered Ethel. "Graduating doesn't mean she can sleep till noon. If she can't get down when the rest of us eat, she can make her own. She can wash the dishes, too. She'll be Little Miss High-Hat after getting that scholarship. Can't have that!"

Julie knocked on Colleen's door and heard her sleepy answer. She opened the door.

"Wow, do you look nice!" said Colleen, sitting up in bed.

Julie was satisfied. She had decided on a royal blue blouse and skirt for the conference with Alex Stewart. Colleen's approval gave her confidence, and she thought how the same color would perk up her sister's drab wardrobe. Her mother wouldn't approve; Ethel thought Colleen too heavy to wear bright colors.

"You won't believe it, but I have a conference today with the man who nearly ran me down," said Julie.

"I *don't* believe it. How come?"

"His daughter is a student at Pennington. She has some disciplinary problems, and she was assigned to me for evaluation and tutoring, if necessary."

"Do you think he'll remember you?"

"I'm sure of it. Last night I plowed right into him at your commencement and fell with the grace of a giraffe. When he sees me, he'll remember," Julie said with a dour look.

Colleen shook with laughter. "I knew it! I knew there would be consequences from that meeting. You were trying too hard to convince yourself he was bad news."

Julie's face flushed, and she yanked her sister's covers off. "Stop giggling and listen to me. Orders are that you get yourself downstairs at once."

Colleen's face sobered. "Is she in a bad mood?"

"When is she not? Get dressed and, for all our sakes, try to keep things peaceful when Dad gets home."

A frown foretold a question from Colleen, and Julie went out the door to avoid it. She wished she had time to explain; it wasn't fair to leave Colleen out. The truth was, she wanted to clear her mind. Duty called, and today she would joust with the dragon.

Chapter 3

Julie's appointment with Alex Stewart was for ten o'clock, and her nerves grew more unsettled as the hour approached. Why? She had dealt with the same situation a hundred times or more.

Picking up a stack of letters on her desk, her mind still meandering, she carried them to the file cabinet. Was she apprehensive because he was a minister? He certainly didn't act the way she thought a minister should, dashing around in his jaunty little sports car and flirting with unattached females.

Julie blinked her eyes and shook her head. Had she actually made a mental note of his car? And the flirting bit — how did that get in there? The only unattached female she knew he'd spoken to was her!

Deliberately, she switched thoughts to her father's escapade the night before. How would her mother react if she knew? Ethel was a spoiled child who never grew up. Even their home was a gift from her parents.

Sid Richmond's upbringing was in stark contrast to Ethel's. He was his family's sole support after his father's death until two years before he married. Knowing about the house, he must have accepted Ethel's insta-bility and left the rest to fate. But fate had been unkind, and her father had chosen an out.

The telephone buzzed. Julie answered, then cleared her desk and placed Amelia's folder before her. The door opened, and Nita, the secretary, stood calf-eyed, gazing up at Alex Stewart.

"Thank you, Nita," said Julie. "Would you bring coffee for us, please? Unless you'd rather have a cold drink?" she asked her guest.

"Coffee's fine, thank you." He smiled at Nita, who left with a rapturous look back at him.

Julie had not risen. It was meant to show him who was in charge. She nodded toward one of the chairs in front of her desk, and Alex Stewart sat down in the chair next to it. Julie's eyes lowered.

"Thank you for being so prompt," she said crisply.

"It was no hardship. My time is valuable, too."

Score one for you, thought Julie. No wit-ticism today. That was good; they could get down to business. She opened the folder.

"I'm trying to understand why Amelia is having difficulty with the rules at Pennington. I'm not sure she's happy here."

"Is that what this is all about?" He sat back. "Because if it is, I'm getting a different story. She likes the school, and she tells me she loves you."

His declaration surprised Julie. Having talked alone with Amelia only twice, she hardly knew her. Why would Amelia tell her father she loved an assistant principal?

"That's puzzling," she said. "It seems she's playing a double role. Her disposition at Pennington is an unruly one."

"In what way?" he asked with a frown.

Julie took her time. "She talks back to her teachers, which encourages other students to do the same. Also, disruptions in her classroom take place on a regular basis."

"Are you saying she provokes trouble?"

Julie felt an explosion building and tempered her reply to defuse it.

"I realize this is upsetting for you, Mr. Stewart, but —"

"Please, call me Alex," he said, clearly trying to handle his feelings.

Nita brought the coffee, and Julie was spared addressing this threat to the reserved manner she'd assumed. When the girl left, Julie poured their coffee. He took it black as she did.

Continuing, she stated, "These incidents

may be occurring because something is bothering Amelia inside. I hope, together, we can discover what it is."

"Yes, of course," murmured Alex.

He was distraught, and Julie had no explanation. Surely this was not unexpected; it was a conference after all. But his next words proved her wrong.

"You'll have to forgive me, Miss Richmond. I'm trying to deal with what you've told me. I love my daughter very much. It's impossible to think of her as a troublemaker.

"My wife left me before Amelia really knew her. I've been both father and mother to her; however, we've always had a good housekeeper," he said as if defending the idea that a hired caregiver was enough.

"What is Amelia's attitude toward the housekeeper?"

"Good, and Mrs. Blake has no complaints either."

Julie felt she was getting nowhere. His attitude was more serious, but he was still aloof, covering up for Amelia's conduct. In any case, she had to forget the father and think of the child.

"Then it's obvious that since other areas of Amelia's life are in order, we need to focus on the problem at school. You say she loves school. On what do you base that?"

"She never tries to skip. In fact, she's enthusiastic."

"All right," Julie said, making a note. "You also said she loves me. How do you know that?"

Alex set his cup on a side table and leaned forward, his elbows on his knees. "She prays for you every night, and she wishes you were her mother."

Julie felt her face warm. She sipped her coffee to keep from looking at him. Being a player in this scenario was not in her plan. It was a few seconds before she found her voice.

"I can't explain her affections for me. Amelia and I haven't been together that much," she countered.

"Maybe not, but what you said or did impressed my daughter to an unusual degree. Since you know how she feels about you, perhaps you can come up with some ideas of your own to help."

Irritated by the suggestion, Julie remembered that their conference was supposed to be for his benefit. He had neatly reversed the roles, and she had to get back on track.

"I will certainly try; although, these things sometimes happen when changes occur in the home." Taking one of her cards from a porcelain box on her desk, she held it out to him. "If you think of anything that might cause Amelia's attitude problem, I'd appreciate your giving me a call."

Alex whipped out his business card. "And I'd appreciate it if you'd do the same."

Julie got up, trembling, and followed him to the door. When she could no longer hear his and Nita's voices, she went to a large window that overlooked the front of the building. Seconds later he strode down the front walk to a modest, late-model automobile. *No sports car today,* she thought. Was he trying to impress her with his down-to-earth persona?

No, that wasn't right. He didn't know she'd seen his car today. At that moment, he turned and waved up at her. Julie backed away from the window, her hands balled into fists.

Seething, she grabbed the coffee tray and carried it to the reception area. Nita took it, her eyes on Julie's face.

"What's wrong, Julie? Didn't it go well?"

"It did not go well! I may as well resolve Amelia Stewart's problem myself — her father certainly isn't any help."

Two teachers listened at the door to the copier room. One was Miss Clay, Amelia's teacher the past year.

"Did you say Amelia Stewart?" she asked. "What now?"

Julie paced up and down. "I just had a talk with *The Reverend.* Alex Stewart, that is."

"You're lucky. I tried, but he was always covered up with appointments or meetings and couldn't come in. Maybe I should have brought my problems to you in the first place."

"No, thanks! I don't want them either. He's impossible!"

Julie's voice had risen, and Mrs. Larabee, their elderly principal, came out of her office.

"Ladies, please. Someone might hear," she cautioned. "May I ask who it is you're discussing?"

"Amelia Stewart's father, ma'am," supplied Julie.

"Oh, yes. A likeable man. A pastor, I believe."

"I'm afraid I don't find him a likeable man. His daughter has problems, and you felt I could work well with Amelia. Since meeting her father, I'm not sure I'm . . ."

"I'm sorry, my dear. I can't give you a choice. We must learn to adapt to difficult situations. Isn't that what we teach our young ladies?"

Julie nodded, and things fell in place.

Mrs. Larabee spoke from years of experience, and, of course, she was right. Julie had to work with Alex if she intended to improve Amelia's deportment.

A week later, Colleen, dressed in jeans and a sweatshirt, was curled up in an armchair, reading. The doorbell rang. She sauntered to the door finishing a paragraph, but when she saw the caller, she wished she'd hurried.

"Curt!"

"Hi, Colleen. Is Lisa home?" the husky blond man asked, looking toward the staircase with hope that was all too obvious.

"No, I'm sorry, she isn't. Would you like to come in and wait?" Regretting the invitation, she said, "Or maybe it would be better to sit in the swing out here." She motioned with her hand.

"I guess the battle lines are drawn since last week, huh?" Ashamed her parents' quarrels were common knowledge, Colleen looked away.

"I can wait awhile, I guess. I have to get back soon though." The swing creaked and swayed forward as he sat down.

"When the days are as nice as they have been this month, I guess it's hard to stay buried in your books all the time."

"Huh? Oh yeah. I have to make myself stay at it."

"You have classes this summer, too, don't you? That doesn't leave much time for girls."

"Right. But I want to see your sister before I leave."

Colleen had heard that Curt and Lisa were together on the night of her graduation, but that night was such a happy one she put them out of her mind. She'd wanted to believe graduation from high school would make Curt notice her. Nothing had changed. To him she was still gorgeous Lisa's plump, uninteresting sister. What did it matter that her IQ was higher than Curt's?

"I guess you're happy about the scholarship to Lindenwood, aren't you? You won't be far from Wash U," he said, obviously making conversation as he peered down the street.

Colleen used the question as an excuse to approach the swing. Grasping the chain, she stilled her quivering hands. She'd never think of sitting beside him unless he asked.

"Yes, it's a good college. I want to go as far as I can in school. Maybe even a doctorate. Look where Julie's master's landed her."

"She's got a cushy job all right. But so has

Lisa," he added quickly.

"Lisa only went to business school."

"I believe in everyone doing his own thing. Four years at a regular college would have bored Lisa."

"I suppose so. She wouldn't have met Mr. Sherry either," she said with a hint that the older man was special to Lisa.

"No, and that would have been a real shame." He missed the innuendo. "Sherry has done a lot for Lisa."

Calling over her shoulder as she headed for the door, Colleen said she hoped he wouldn't have to wait too long. Inside, a sarcastic quarrel held sway in the kitchen, and she ran quietly up the stairs to her room.

Leaning against the closed door, she scrubbed at her eyes as she cried for long, anguished minutes. How could Curt be so blind? She loved him far more than Lisa did.

In less than three months she'd leave for Lindenwood, at St. Charles. As he'd said, she would be close to his school in St. Louis. A lot of good that would do; he couldn't even see her when they were face-to-face.

Nagging her memory was what Curt said about the battle lines being drawn *since last week*. What did he mean? Lisa knew, and if Lisa knew, so did Julie. Colleen wished for Julie. She needed a shoulder to cry on. And she needed to know what Curt was talking about.

Amelia's problems might be related to her academic work, so Julie started with her reading skills. She had a library of books she'd like to introduce to the child, but they should focus on the right subject. Amelia would read what she was most interested in.

She called Alex's house to make an appointment for time with the little girl. Expecting the housekeeper to answer, she was surprised when Alex picked up the phone.

"This is Julie Richmond."

"I know," he said softly.

Julie felt the air getting thin. "I called to talk about Amelia's choice of literature, and to ask if I might spend some time with her next week."

"Spending time with her is a great idea, but I'm afraid I can't tell you what she likes to read. I don't see her reading anything except her lessons for Sunday school."

"Do you have to make her read those?"

"Not exactly. She knows they're required for her class. It's the scaled-down version of our Bible study."

"But she has no shelf of books in her room that she escapes to occasionally?"

"No. Should I go out and select some books for her?"

"I'd rather Amelia did that. I'd like to see her on Tuesday afternoon. Would it be convenient to drop her off at school around one o'clock?"

"Certainly. I appreciate this, Miss Richmond, and I apologize for being so unmovable at our first interview. It's hard for a parent to face any imperfection in his child."

"I understand. But the first consideration should be your daughter. Our personal feelings are not important."

His chuckle brought back the memory of her inelegant fall at the auditorium, and she caught herself, mouth open, ready to give him a stinging résumé of his character.

Once she was off the phone, Julie calmed down. Their conversation had told her a lot. Alex probably ignored all but the spiritual side of Amelia's needs. And what about her report cards? Didn't he look at them? He knew neither what she liked to read nor her ability or comprehension. On top of that, his offer to supply the child with reading material meant merely filling a bookshelf. Didn't he spend any time with her at all?

Julie put Amelia's folder in the file cabinet, wondering about her exposure to

49

music and the other arts. Had she ever seen a play or a concert, or visited an art gallery or museum? She made up her mind. This summer, Amelia Stewart would be introduced to the world of the senses: sight, sound, touch, taste, and smell. Julie would make up for Alex's oversight.

Amelia Stewart bounced up the walk below Julie's window, and her father watched her until she was in the building, out of his sight. This time he did not check her window, Julie noticed. His total attention was on his daughter.

In seconds, Amelia knocked on her office door. Julie answered with a smile and invited the tiny brunette in. Her resemblance to Alex was startling. Her nose had not yet taken on the straight line of her father's; but her lips were full like his, and the same smile danced in her brown eyes. Julie couldn't believe she had noticed that many features of the man.

Still smiling, Julie led Amelia to a tea table she had ready. When she learned of Julie's plan, Mrs. Larabee had loaned her the mahogany table and English bone china tea set usually found in a corner of the principal's office. She also sent along demitasse silver, an Irish-linen tablecloth, and spice tea Julie knew was a favorite at Pennington. Mrs. Larabee's consideration was a distinct privilege.

It was immediately apparent that Amelia needed work on table manners. Yet as she absorbed Julie's suggestions, she showed finesse even Mrs. Larabee would approve of. Later, Julie got to the purpose of the afternoon.

"Amelia, it's Pennington's goal that every girl be taught poise and grace that will stay with her all her life." She explained both words to Amelia and continued, "We spend time with girls during the summer helping them reach that goal. You and I will be doing that this year. I hope you will enjoy it as much as I plan to."

"Oh, I will, Miss Richmond. I know I will." Amelia's eyes passed over the dainty plates of party sandwiches and lemon cookies, and the graceful teapot with its thin cups and saucers. Folding her napkin and spreading her hands in an outward gesture, she said, "I've never done anything like this before, and it was so nice."

In her mind Julie heard Colleen voicing similar words. *Alex and I have the same problem,* she thought. *We have deprived young people in both our homes, and it's not any more his fault than it is mine.* It startled her that she'd seen his side.

Opening the glass doors of an oak book-case, Julie brought out a colorful book about a girl who wanted to be the queen of her country. Along with royal functions she thought so grand, the girl learned that a queen had responsibilities that must be carried out whether she felt like it or not.

Amelia expressed her gratitude with wide eyes. "I'll take good care of this book. You wait and see."

"I know you will, honey."

Julie pulled Amelia to her and gave her a hug just as Alex opened the door gently to look inside. The tender look he gave her almost melted Julie's heart. Almost. She straightened her shoulders and lifted her chin.

"Look who's here, Amelia," said Miss Richmond.

Chapter 4

Her father would be in from his territory that night. Though learning her new job at the branch library, Colleen had not forgotten that Lisa and Julie were keeping something from her. When she got home from work, Lisa was in her room, and Julie came home shortly afterward.

Beckoning to Lisa, Colleen headed down the hall toward Julie's room. Lisa hung up the dress she was holding and joined her.

"Have you lost your voice?" she asked.

"No, I don't want Mother to hear," Colleen murmured.

Julie stepped out into the hall. "She's downstairs. What's all the whispering about?"

Colleen herded the other two into Julie's room. Painted a warm ivory highlighted with forest green, impudent touches of gold and hot pink spoke of a free spirit in residence.

Colleen sat on the floor, leaned back against the wall, and waited until she had the attention of the other two. With a deep breath, she plunged in.

"Curt said something he didn't mean to

the other night, and I want to know what's going on with the folks."

Julie looked at Lisa, who shrugged and dropped down to sit on Julie's cedar chest. She told Colleen the whole story. Colleen felt like crying, but she didn't.

"I'd heard some talk. I didn't want to believe Dad could be unfaithful, so I told myself they were wrong," she said in a choked voice. "But deep in my heart, I knew."

"That was a big load for you to carry, honey. Why didn't you tell one of us?" asked Julie, moving to sit beside Colleen.

"I thought if I kept it to myself, he might stop, and I wouldn't have to tell."

"Wish for the moon, Colleen," Lisa muttered. "What incentive does he have to stop? I've thought about this, and I can almost forgive him for wanting someone to love him. Mother sure doesn't, or at least she's never shown it."

"I guess I don't show much love for either of them," Colleen confessed.

"That goes for all of us," said Julie. "But let's face it, they're a hard couple to love. They've taught me one thing, though. Either get married and keep working at it, or don't get married at all. As for me," she declared, "I choose the latter."

Now was not the time to argue. Colleen concentrated on the problem at hand.

"I guess my next question is, does Mother suspect anything, and are we going to tell her? I vote no."

"I don't have the nerve either," said Lisa.

A sound at the door caused all three to turn. Ethel, her face pale, stood staring straight ahead. Knowing she'd heard their conversation, Colleen rushed to her mother as she slid down along the doorframe in a faint. Julie helped lay her down, and Lisa dashed to the bathroom for a wet washcloth.

"Do you think she overheard us?" she asked, folding the cloth and pressing it to her mother's forehead.

"Every word," said Julie. "How could we be so cruel?"

Colleen heard regret in Julie's voice; she was the family conscience. She gave them more direction than their parents.

"I never dreamed she'd take it like this," Colleen murmured. "What should we do?"

No one answered. Lisa grabbed a bed pillow, and Colleen helped place it under her mother's head. Julie covered her with a fleece blanket from her cedar chest.

"Shouldn't we call an ambulance or a doctor?" Colleen asked.

Ethel moaned and muttered indistinct

words. Colleen knelt and took her hand.

"Mother, it's Colleen. Are you all right?"

Ethel's eyes traveled from one to the other. Her face wore a dazed, then a bitter expression.

"So you all knew about it. Everyone but me." The bitter expression changed to one of self-pity. "Why am I being punished like this? Lisa, you say you understand Sid wanting someone to love him. What about me? I need love, too; instead, he made a fool of me with another woman."

Brittle silence enveloped the room. *No one knows what to say,* thought Colleen. Minutes passed with Ethel mumbling, sometimes incoherently. Julie asked if she wanted to sit up or lie on her bed, and Ethel ordered them to help her to her bedroom. She wanted to be alone, she said, and the girls left.

Casting a backward glance, Colleen wondered if their mother should be by herself.

"She wouldn't try to . . ." Colleen couldn't finish. "Would she?" she whispered.

"No," said Julie, "I think she's adjusting to the shock. I'll check on her in a little while, though."

Colleen tried to remember. Was anything in her parents' medicine chest lethal? Ethel was a hypochondriac; she might have several medications that could end her life. But would she have the nerve? As Julie said, probably not. Once her mother absorbed what she'd heard, she'd scream and shout, but then she'd think of something more appropriate, Colleen decided. She might even lock her wayward husband out of the house.

Lisa and Julie made for the front porch, and she followed. Lisa propped herself against the porch railing while the other two occupied the swing. Sounds of twilight surrounded them.

"We've forced ourselves into a corner," said Julie. "We have to come up with some sort of strategy."

"Dad's supposed to come in tonight. Shouldn't we hear his side of the story before he sees Mother?" asked Colleen.

"Do you honestly think he'd talk to us?"

"Wait, Lisa! She might have something," said Julie with enthusiasm. "There's going to be a blowup the minute he and Mother meet. Let's try pounding some sense into his head before he talks to her. Maybe he hasn't considered how this affects all of us. After all it's our home, too. Aren't we entitled to try to hold it together?"

Good, thought Colleen. Julie was for it. Talking to their father might not work, but it was worth a try.

Sid did not show up that night at all. The next morning Ethel was so upset Lisa faked a headache, called Leonard Sherry, and took the day off. Assuring her one of them would waylay Sid before he clashed with Ethel, Julie dropped Colleen at the library on her way to Pennington.

At school, she checked her calendar to see which day of her busy week allowed time with Amelia. Regardless of the family situation, the child was her project for the next six weeks. Every day, except that afternoon, was full. She called the Stewart home, got permission from the housekeeper to take Amelia to a children's play, and picked her up a little after noon.

"Daddy said you'd call me, Miss Richmond," Amelia chattered as she pranced down the walk to the car. "But I was afraid it would be like when *he* says we'll go somewhere and we don't. You know what he did when I told him that? He got down on one knee beside me, real frowny, and said, 'Do I do that, my little girl?' and I almost cried."

Another score for Alex, thought Julie. Mrs. Blake was still at the front door, smiling and waving good-bye to Amelia. The housekeeper did love the child. No doubt she did her best, but she was not

Amelia's mother or grandmother; and the disparity in their ages might inhibit real closeness.

The afternoon went well. Amelia was delighted with the play and wanted to relive every scene.

"Wasn't it beautiful when all the trees bowed down to the boy and girl, and the fairy came out of the sky all sparkles?" she asked. "I think I know what I'd like to be when I grow up. An actress! Yes, that's what I want to be."

"Then you need to read all the books you can because books, called scripts, are what plays are made of," said Julie. "Also, it would be a good idea to try out for the school play next year. That would help you decide if you like performing."

Amelia's expression darkened, and Julie knew she had hit on something.

"I probably wouldn't get a part. Caroline Basset gets all the main parts," she said with a sour voice.

"But wouldn't you be satisfied with another part instead of the main one? Sometimes it's those characters people remember."

"No! If I can't have the main part, I don't want to be in the old play."

A big fat clue to her attitude, thought Julie. "Did you read the book I loaned you?" she asked, dismissing the play.

"Yes, Miss Richmond, and I liked it. May I borrow another one?" Amelia's face was sunny again.

Julie turned onto Vivion and parked at a Baskin-Robbins ice cream shop. Inside, she ordered two small dishes of sherbet. Above them hung a cluster of pink balloons, and the boy at the counter told Amelia she could have one when she left. The child thanked him and popped a spoonful of sherbet into her mouth as soon as she sat down.

"Oh, it's so good," Amelia commented, using her napkin and good manners. "You have the best ideas, Miss Richmond."

"I don't think sherbet will spoil your appetite for dinner. Mrs. Blake wouldn't like that, I'm afraid."

"She wouldn't care, and neither would Daddy. They never scold."

And so your classmates suffer because you're never told no at home, thought Julie. Could this angelic child, dressed in white lace stockings and a candy-striped dress be a tyrant? With no knowledge of how to be less than number one, she got her way at school by causing turmoil and manipulating her classmates. Likewise, if she couldn't be the star of the school play, she wouldn't try at all.

Back in the car, Amelia's pink balloon bounced above her head while she charmed Julie all the way home. The car Julie had seen Alex get into at the school was parked in the drive. As they pulled up, Alex came out of the house with an expression so serious Julie wondered if he was angry with her for taking Amelia to the play. Surely Mrs. Blake had cleared it with him when Julie called about picking her up.

He opened Amelia's door, gave her a kiss, and sent her away with her balloon. Amelia waved to Julie when she reached the stoop of the modest ranch-style home.

"Don't tell me I've kept her out too late?"

"No, Julie, and I want you to remember how grateful I am that you've taken time to be with my daughter."

As he got into the passenger seat beside her, Julie wondered why he had used her given name and why his mood was so grave.

"Wh–What is it?" she stammered.

Alex settled back and studied her face. "There was a fire near my church last night. A motel burned, and three people died. I was called, and as soon as I knew the church property was in no danger, I went over to see if I could help." Alex took her hand. "An hour ago, they made a positive identification of one of the men." With his other hand on her shoulder, he turned her to face him. "It was your father, Julie," he said gently.

His voice seemed to get farther and farther away. Was she going to faint? *No*. She couldn't; she had to pull herself together and find out more. She was trembling, but her voice was as firm as she could make it.

"Does my family know?"

"Not yet. They let me come here because I wanted to be the one to tell you. The police will be at your house any minute. If you'd like me to, I'll come around and drive you home to be with your family."

Julie wanted to be in control, but she was shaking so that any fool could see she was not. Then the worst thing in the world happened. Alex pulled her to him, and her defense against tears crumbled. As he held her, stroking her hair, comforting her with words he might use with Amelia, she cried for herself and Lisa and Colleen, and for their mother.

Chapter 5

Lisa had a real headache after spending all day with her mother. She wasn't harassed, but the fact that she wasn't caused the tension. Ethel consented to eat a light supper, and Lisa had taken it upstairs. She was coming down when, outside, she saw a man, at least six-foot-four, open the door of Julie's car and help her out. It was inconceivable. Julie was hanging onto a man! And a handsome one at that.

Then an even stranger thing occurred. A police car drew up to the curb. Julie, the man she was with, and two policemen spoke together for a moment, then all four walked toward the house.

As they neared the front door, Lisa's impish demeanor changed to one of fear. The man with Julie opened the screen door as Lisa made herself walk toward them.

"I'm Alex Stewart. I'm —"

"Excuse me, Alex," Julie said with an awkward movement of her hand. "This is my sister Lisa."

Alex remembered his manners. "Lisa, I'm glad to know you. These men are here on official business." But Alex's concern was for

Julie. He walked her to the living room couch, still holding her hand. "Julie will be all right. She's had a shock, and I'm afraid it will be one for you."

When the policemen broke the news about her father, Lisa listened and started to cry, sending Julie to her side. Alex rose, too, but an older woman at the head of the stairs caught his attention. Her face reflected anger beyond reason.

"Who are you?" she snapped at Alex. "What's going on down there? Girls! What are these men doing here? And what have you done to Lisa, Julie? Why is she crying?"

Alex was baffled by the woman's attitude. Julie had cried all the way home, and her beautiful face was cheerless and swollen. The older woman, maybe even her mother, was castigating her before she even knew what had happened. The two officers stared at Alex as if he should be able to explain.

"My name is Reverend Alex Stewart. I'm a friend of Julie's," he said, addressing the woman on the stairs.

One of the officers spoke up, "These ladies have received some bad news, ma'am. Are you Mrs. Sidney Richmond?"

Ethel nodded. She tottered and seemed to lose strength. Alex leaped up the stairs to support her, but Ethel shrugged off his help.

He followed her determined stride down the stairs.

"What happened?" she screeched at Julie. "Did he run off with that woman?"

Still trying to make sense of the mother's attitude and her scorching questions leveled at Julie, Alex intervened.

"Why don't you have a seat, Mrs. Richmond," he suggested. "These officers will give you the details you want."

"Such as?" she spat at the policemen.

Alex watched the woman's face as the facts were reiterated. Her mouth screwed up like that of an aged crone, and she crumpled into a chair, her face in her hands. Julie spoke gently to her, but Ethel waved her off and called Lisa's name. As Lisa put her arm around her, Julie stood back, embarrassed.

It's because we're here, thought Alex. He suspected this happened often but not in front of strangers. He wanted to hold Julie and comfort her, yet he doubted she'd allow it. Instead, he took her arm and guided her outside.

"Let's sit in the swing," he said stoutly, not giving her a chance to refuse.

Julie sank into the seat of the swing, her shoulders slumped. Alex's arm dropped to the back of the swing behind her, and she didn't object. The evening had cooled, and

Alex wondered if she merely welcomed his warmth. They rocked back and forth, listening to the muffled voices of the officers, Ethel's wails of self-pity, and the plaintive pleas for calm by Lisa. Julie's head rested against Alex's arm, and he was surprised but happy it was there.

A small, plump teenager with a stack of books in her arms strode down the street and turned onto the walk. There was no mistaking the family resemblance. It was Julie's sister, who had given the valedictory speech at Kinner High.

"Julie?" The girl hurried up the steps and set her books on the porch railing. One fell off. "Julie, what's wrong? Why are you crying?"

Alex retrieved the book as the girl sat beside Julie. Her voice trembling, Julie introduced them. Colleen pulled her skirt aside so Alex could sit down again.

Once more, he watched a Richmond daughter cave in at the news. Yet Colleen seemed to be mature enough to take it, he noticed. Clinging to Julie, she made no move to go inside, though her mother's frequent outcries were heard. Some were against the dead man, and Alex remembered what he'd heard earlier.

It wasn't the only thing he questioned.

Why would a man, even a salesman who traveled a lot, be in a motel so close to his home? Was there more truth to Ethel Richmond's accusations than the others wanted him to know? Not one had mentioned another woman.

Ethel insisted on seeing Sid's body. She got as far as the police morgue before passing out. Alex had offered to go with Ethel and Julie, and Julie accepted, more thankful than she cared to admit. When Ethel was herself again, Alex took her back to the car to wait.

Julie signed the necessary documentation, then clung to Alex's arm, drawing from his strength, until she could escape the place. On the way home she distanced herself from him again to regain her confidence.

Ethel went up to her room at once. Julie thanked Alex and offered a half-hearted invitation to stay for coffee. He accepted. In the old-fashioned kitchen, somewhat redeemed by a partial face-lift of the cabinets, Julie filled the coffeemaker and joined Alex at the table to wait.

"I suppose you realize by now that my father was seeing another woman. In his defense, I have to tell you — my mother is not the easiest person in the world to live with."

"She was a little testy when I first met her," said Alex. "But why does she give such latitude to Lisa and none to you?"

Julie blushed when she realized he'd picked up on a fact she'd tried to rationalize since childhood. She gave him what was, to her, the only answer.

"Lisa is so beautiful it's difficult for anyone to deny her preeminence."

Alex snorted. "Wait a minute. Is it possible you think Lisa is more beautiful than you are?"

Julie swept him a derisive look. "Don't try to flatter me, Alex. I haven't lived in Lisa's shadow for twenty-one years without realizing that."

"Who did the judging? Your mother? Your father? Lisa? Somehow I don't think Colleen falls in the group. She probably thinks you're as pretty as I do."

The shield around Julie's heart dropped abruptly into place. She was too smart to fall prey to a few compliments. Look where she was now, and all because of a man. Everything she had worked for was in jeopardy; her father's scandal and manner of death could cause her immediate termination at socially conscious Pennington.

She had no idea what would happen to

her mother. Ethel had teetered on the edge of, yes, *madness,* for years. With her unnatural exhibitions of temper, grudges followed by violent acts of revenge, and contempt for everyone except Lisa, she couldn't manage what had happened.

Julie realized she must be stronger than ever. She would hold them together, through the embarrassment, through the funeral, and through the beginning of life without Sid. They would survive.

Alex listened to the silence and knew he'd made a mistake.

If he wanted to remain close to her, he would have to go slow. Julie's independent self wouldn't be smothered, and she didn't trust men because of her parents' tragic marriage. He understood, but it saddened him. God had the answer to her doubts, but it would be a long time before she was ready to believe that.

Two days after his death, Sid was buried. Ethel didn't care who officiated, and, knowing no other minister, Julie asked Alex to conduct the graveside service. The story was carried in the newspapers, but Ethel refused to have them in the house. Julie didn't need reminding either.

The insurance company had no Sid Richmond on its books. Aghast, Julie asked Lisa to investigate; surely, it was a mistake. Lisa came home angrier than Julie had ever seen her.

"Do you want to know the meaning of *rat?* I'll tell you the meaning of rat! It's a father who cancels his life insurance without telling his family. Two years ago! Can you believe it? A hundred-thousand-dollar policy, and he cancels it! Who do you think he spent the payment money on?"

Julie couldn't speak. Nothing substantial would come from Sid's company. He had used up his savings plan. She might soon be jobless, Colleen would need help with college, and the house and cars had to be maintained. With his secret life her father had plundered their future security without a thought for his family.

After shopping for books to begin Amelia's own library, Julie dropped her off at the huge red-brick building that was Alex's church. From a side door, he waved her down, trotted out to her car, and opened her door.

"Can you come in for a few minutes? I need to talk to you."

Julie drove into the nearest parking slot, and Amelia gave her a hug and left for a children's choir rehearsal. Alex guided Julie through the church labyrinth to his office.

It was a pleasant room, full of light. With floor-to-ceiling bookshelves, green plants beside a row of file cabinets, a huge desk with a computer monitor to one side, the office looked organized and ready for business. Why had she hoped it would be messy?

Once they were in comfortable leather chairs opposite each other, Alex apologized. "I'm sorry I can't offer you coffee. My next appointment doesn't like the smell." He sat back and sighed. "I have something to tell you." Then looking into Julie's eyes, he said, "The woman who was with your father was badly burned and has been in the hospital since the fire. I went to see her, Julie. She wanted me to tell you she's sorry for everything that happened."

Seething with anger, Julie stood up. Like a toy soldier, she walked rigidly to a window looking out on the parking lot. Her voice would hardly obey her brain.

"You can tell me that after the torment my family has been through? After what we may all go through yet?" She whirled to face him. "How could you do that? Tell me, *please!*"

"She's a poor, lost soul, Julie," he said, moving toward her.

"Are we talking souls that go to heaven or hell, or are we talking slimy souls that rob a family of decency and . . . and feed on innocent victims?"

"We're talking souls Jesus Christ died for," Alex said calmly.

"Oh! Yes." Julie laughed. "I forgot. Here comes the commercial."

"No, I'm trying to explain my position. Please, Julie, try to understand. Regardless of what people do, Jesus loves them. My aim in life is to reach everyone I meet with that message. You may not believe it, or care, but that woman did ask His forgiveness, and she accepted Christ as her Savior."

"Thank you very much, I appreciate the sermon, good-bye."

Rushing to the door, Julie opened it to see the upraised hand of a tall, unpleasant-looking woman about to knock.

"Please, Julie, don't leave like this," Alex pleaded, not at an angle to see the visitor.

"Well, really, Dr. Stewart! I can see now why my appointment was dealt with so casually," the woman chided, glancing at her watch. "I was supposed to see you six minutes ago, and I've been waiting since."

Alex's face held such distress Julie felt avenged. *Let his reputation take a few hits*, she thought as she dashed out.

"Mrs. Biddle, please, be seated. I will be right with you."

He hurried after Julie, who couldn't, for the life of her, remember the door they'd entered. He caught up with her, grabbed her arm, and spun her around. She thumped against his chest.

"Now you listen to me, young lady," he demanded softly. "I'm a minister. You learned that shortly after we met. But ministers fall in love just like everyone else." He put his other arm around her and loosened his grip on the arm he held. "I think I'm falling in love with you, Julie," he finished.

Behind them, Mrs. Biddle gasped. "Well! This is too much! Forget my appointment, Dr. Stewart!" Her heels clicked down a hallway out of their hearing.

"Great PR, *Doctor*. Any more surprises up your sleeve? How about your wife? You said she left you, but I haven't heard anything about a divorce."

"My wife died, Julie. It's easier for me to say she left. As for the 'doctor' bit, it's an honorary degree. I don't use the title because I didn't work for it. Like you, I have a master's. Mrs. Biddle is one of the few who addresses me as doctor."

With so much coming at once, Julie lost track of the crux of their disagreement. She knew she must get away from Alex before something happened they would both be sorry for. She wasn't ready for his commitment. Not at all!

"I suppose I should thank you, but I wouldn't mean it. If you'll let me go, I'll try to find my way out of here before any more of your *parishioners* check up on you," Julie spat.

"You may think that's funny, but that particular lady has a penchant for telephoning. By tonight's meeting here, a lot of people will know that I was holding beautiful Julie Richmond in my arms today, *in the church!*

"That's unforgivable, eh?"

"To everyone but my Savior."

"No more sermons, Doc. I'm immune!" she said as she stepped away from him. "Tell Amelia I'll call when I can."

Julie went through the door he indicated finally, and the exit was straight ahead.

In a private conversation, Mrs. Larabee told Julie she was given a leave of absence "to come to terms with your tragedy and to decide what is best for your career." It was a cold sentence, and Julie held little hope she would be invited back. As she left the school, she felt as lost as a child in a dark wood.

Her mother had no questions when Julie returned home an hour after she left. Ethel moved from room to room like a ghost with no interest in the day's happenings. She had listened docilely to Lisa's explanation of the insurance and the Social Security checks she was entitled to. But as long as there was food to eat and her bed was available, Ethel cared about nothing else. Julie and her sisters worried that her mind was slipping away.

Not having seen or spoken to Amelia since shopping for her books, Julie felt guilty. Their great summer together was shattered by circumstances out of her control. One night Amelia called, but before Julie could get to the phone, Ethel made a vague excuse and hung up on her. Alex came to the house about ten o'clock that night.

"If I promise not to lay a hand on you or mention God's name, will you go out with me for a cup of coffee?"

They were on the porch, and Julie was hugging herself to keep from trembling.

"Aren't you afraid one of your *flock* will see us and tell?"

"I never was. But, as things stand now, it may no longer matter, in this church anyway."

75

"What do you mean?" Julie asked, aware he was sharing something close to his heart.

"I'm answering letters from other churches that have invited me to preach for them in the past."

"Why?" Her heart beat faster.

"Mrs. Biddle escalated our disagreement in the hall to a torrid love scene, and some of my people believed her."

Her eyes teary, she turned away. "I'm sorry, Alex, honestly."

Alex moved behind her and said in her ear, "Stop it, Julie. Think. We did nothing wrong. God knows it, and that's all that matters. This is in His hands now. If He wants me to stay here, I'll stay; if He doesn't, I won't. He's in control of my life, not people."

Moving away, Julie turned to face him. "I suppose you'd say I could use some faith. I may no longer have a job either. I'm on what's being called a leave of absence, but I doubt they'll ask me back."

Alex pulled her into his arms. "Marry me, Julie."

Twisting, trying to get away, she protested, "Don't be ridiculous! Marriage is the last thing I need! Do you think I want to end up like my mother?"

"No, and I don't want that either. Stand

still, Julie," he commanded with such firm-
ness she stopped struggling.

"Marriage is given by God; it's not meant
to be lived the way your parents did. I'm not
saying we should be married right away. We
have things to work out. But, please, won't
you think about it? I want you as my wife
and Amelia's mother."

Julie clawed her way free. "Amelia? How
dare you! Men will use anything to get their
way. Even a child." Her hands were fists at
her sides. "You're not using *me*, Alex. Marriage wouldn't mend your life any more
than it would mine!"

Alex started to leave. Turning, he looked
back. "I had no idea I would ask this tonight.
Someday, but not tonight. I only want to
take care of you. Remember that, and that I
love you."

He left. Julie couldn't understand why
she was crying.

Chapter 6

Lisa's fingers flew over the computer keys, yet her mind wandered even as she produced letters and legal forms without error. Len said she was the best secretary in the building. With him in mind, Lisa took stock of her alternatives.

Julie would take no vacation that summer, Lisa was sure. It was not a time for the women to be separated; they were still resonating from shock. Reluctant as Lisa was to admit it, Julie managed the house admirably. Repairs and chores Sid had attended to, she hired done at less expense and inconvenience than when he was in charge.

It was the same with the bills and checkbook that, for obvious reasons, Sid had allowed no one else to touch. He made the household accounts sound so complex, Lisa and Julie were astonished at how simple they turned out to be.

Everything had changed, and Lisa was contemplating a different future. Curt was not the romantic knight she had daydreamed about, and he was barely a year older than she. He would have no real money until he became an established doctor, and that could take years. His family was well off, which meant an inheritance, but much farther down the road.

And Curt was skittish about taking money from his parents for expenses he thought unnecessary. They went to inexpensive places to eat, instead of the fine restaurants Len could afford, and they sat in the balcony instead of the orchestra seats on a rare *dress-up* date.

No, it simply wasn't practical to pursue Curt any longer. Colleen could have him, Lisa decided. Her opportunities lay with Leonard Sherry. Although he was nearly twice her age, he was still impressive.

Len wasn't tall like Alex Stewart, but he wasn't overweight as some men were at forty-one. His graying hair, too, had a certain appeal. Lisa didn't think of him as a handsome man, but his prowess in a courtroom was awesome. As Leonard Sherry's wife she would enjoy influence and attention from every quarter.

She had been in his home more than once. It was staffed by a group of devoted servants and was a showplace, reeking of old money and tradition. There was one drawback: Len's disabled mother occupied a suite of rooms, upstairs in one wing of the house. He rarely mentioned her, so Lisa believed she usually kept to herself and would present no problem.

Once she saw the unbalanced scale of assets as a Sherry versus the liabilities as a Richmond, she opted for a plan to marry. It took hardly any effort on her part, and she marched into the Richmond house one night wearing an ostentatious emerald-cut diamond.

Julie was ready for bed when she heard Ethel's whoop of joy. Running down the hall with Colleen, Julie didn't know what to expect. Her mother seemed to have forgotten how to laugh; she must be hysterical. They burst into the room and saw Ethel dancing foolishly around Lisa. Posing in an occasional chair, Lisa crossed her legs and propped her left hand on her knee to display the diamond.

"Wanna see what Len gave me when I promised to marry him?"

Colleen flew to Lisa. "Let me see! Let me see!" she squealed as she grabbed her hand. "Oh, Julie, come look. It's dazzling!"

"Yes, indeed, professor. See what can be done with brains *and* beauty?" bragged Ethel. "Don't you wish you had what it takes to succeed?" Then she muttered bitterly, "Lisa's everything I could have been if you hadn't . . ."

Colleen backed up to stand with Julie. "Mother, why do you always criticize Julie? Whether it's good or bad, you use everything to harass her."

"You watch your tongue, little fatty, or you'll find yourself with fewer privileges!"

"And what would those be, Mother? She has hardly any, now." Julie's eyes glinted with anger.

Her mother put on a pathetic face. "Don't let her hurt me, Lisa," she whined. "She wants to. Look at her!"

Lisa lashed out in fury, "That's ridiculous! Julie would never do such a thing. It's wrong of you to accuse her. She and I don't always see things the same way, but we love each other. Stop trying to come between my sisters and me!" Lisa walked toward the hall. "If I had any qualms about marrying Len, you've cleared my mind, Mother. I'll do anything to get out of this house."

Julie knew it was true. She didn't think Lisa was in love with Len; she was fed up with her life at home, and he was the quickest way out. But he was rich and could afford the lifestyle Lisa wanted.

She heard a soft sound beside her and realized Colleen was crying. Listening to Lisa had, for the moment, chased her mother's hateful remark from Julie's mind. Calling Colleen "little fatty" was characteristic of Ethel's cruelty. Julie put her arm around her sister and led her from the room.

"Honey, don't let Mother hurt you," Julie begged. "I don't know why she takes pleasure in tormenting you and me; but she is our mother, and we're responsible for her. I try to do what I can to —"

"Julie, I know," Colleen interrupted. "You're always sweet to make up for her."

"It doesn't take away the hurt, though, does it? In fact, I seem to add to the fracas. But you'll be leaving for school in a few weeks; you'll be free to live a normal life."

"I can't wait," Colleen replied passionately. They passed Lisa's closed door. "Poor Lisa. What a celebration for her engagement."

Julie smiled slyly. "Maybe we should take her out?" she suggested, raising her eyebrows.

"Lets!" Colleen opened Lisa's door, and they slipped inside.

"We're breakin' out of this joint, baby," Julie murmured, in an imitation of Bogie. Then she smiled. "See how quick you can get ready. We'll take you for a little celebration."

Lisa was already grinning. Julie and Colleen dressed in jeans and pullovers, and, leaving a note for Ethel if she cared to read it, they left the house and got in Julie's car.

At a quick-stop market, Alex backed out of a parking space. He glimpsed a car traveling along the street that looked exactly like Julie's, and curiosity induced him to follow. It was Julie, and her sisters were with her. The girls stopped at an all-night restaurant and jumped out of the car, laughing.

Alex wanted to join them, but he could still hear Julie's angry rejection of his proposal when they last met. He parked his car out of their view and watched for a few seconds. Julie looked wonderful. Still maintaining her independence, she'd made the best of tragedy and helped her sisters do the same.

He couldn't resist being with her. A couple came out the door as he went in, and for a few minutes he and the girls were the only customers. He caught Julie's eye almost immediately. Her look of expectation surprised him. Following her gaze, Lisa and Colleen waved him over, and Alex slid into the booth next to Colleen and opposite Julie.

"We meet under different circumstances,

Alex," said Lisa. "This time we're celebrating. I planned to call you later."

"What's happening?" he asked.

Colleen smiled. "Wedding bells are starting to peal."

Alex's expression changed, and he looked quickly at Julie.

"No, not me," she said. "I'm against such rituals. It's our beautiful Lisa. Show him the hardware, sis."

Lisa shook her left hand before Alex, and he covered his eyes, palms out. Remarking that it was a shame the man couldn't afford something nice, Alex then said he knew Leonard Sherry to speak to and approved of her choice. No one offered Ethel's opinion, and he didn't ask.

The conversation remained light, and Alex enjoyed himself more than he had since the rotten business came up about his holding Julie in his arms at the church. In the meantime, several of the older deacons had begged Alex not to do anything rash. His spiritual integrity would prove itself to the membership, they said, and Alex decided to wait.

"How is Amelia, Alex?" Julie couldn't keep from asking.

"Reading as if there's no tomorrow."

Alex's smile ended. What a time to get

melancholy, he thought. *Will I never let go of the possibility?* He'd had Amelia's heart examined again early yesterday; he'd make an invalid of her if he didn't stop watching her so closely. Because Christi died of heart disease didn't mean their daughter would inherit it. Nevertheless, he would not let it slip up on her the way it had Christi.

"Let's call this meeting to order, parson," Lisa teased. "I want you to perform the ceremony. Consult your calendar, and give me some open dates."

Julie's eyes were locked on him, and Alex was uneasy. Had she noticed his change of mood, or was she against his doing the wedding? The latter question had to be answered sooner or later; it might as well be now.

"I'd consider it an honor to perform your marriage ceremony, Lisa." Julie dropped her eyes, so he was unable to see the effect of his answer. "I will check my calendar and let you know as soon as possible. In the meantime, you might advise me of the size of the wedding and where it will take place."

"If Lisa is sure she wants to do this, I'd like to have it for them in our home," Julie interjected, and Alex wondered if she was against Lisa's marrying or if she was against her marrying an older man.

Lisa gave Julie a quick glance. "I'll have to talk to Len about that, Julie. He may want the wedding in his home. After all, a lot of his friends will be invited, and our house might not hold them all."

Julie said nothing, but it was clear to Alex that Lisa did not want her wedding at the Richmond home. Hoping Lisa's reply hadn't hurt Julie, he tried a diplomatic suggestion.

"I'd like to offer the facilities of my church if you want to think about that. If the sanctuary is free on the date you select, you can have it. If not, we have a chapel, which was the original sanctuary before we outgrew it. It's very nice and seats about two hundred," he said.

"I'd like a home wedding, especially at his home, but if Len wants to use your church, I'll let you know soon. Now, who wants to join me for chocolate mousse?"

Julie unlocked the car, and they got in. She noticed Alex waited until their car was on the street before he drove off in the opposite direction.

"I thought you were going to choke when I asked Alex to do the ceremony," said Lisa. "I thought you liked him. He's the only minister we know, and I didn't think you'd mind if he did the honors."

"I don't," answered Julie. "It's just that Alex and I didn't part on the best of terms the last time we met."

In the backseat, Colleen leaned forward to get in on the conversation.

"I didn't know that, Julie, what happened?"

Julie could feel her face turning red. "It was personal, honey."

"Ooh, personal, eh?" Lisa quizzed. "Not even about Amelia. Just personal. *Verrry* interesting."

"Cut it out. I'm not saying any more."

Lisa sniffed and sat back in the passenger seat. "Shame. I'll just have to ask Alex."

Julie stepped on the brake. "Lisa Richmond, if you dare —"

"Don't worry," interrupted Lisa. "Your secret's safe with me."

"What secret? That's not fair. Let me in on this," begged Colleen.

"There is nothing to be let in on. I stand foursquare against marriage — always have, always will," vowed Julie.

"Famous last words," giggled Lisa, looking at Colleen.

Julie didn't even want to see Colleen's face.

★ ★ ★

Len Sherry did want the wedding in his home for his mother's convenience. Lisa was relieved. She knew Julie would put on a beautiful wedding, but Lisa wanted something better. Ethel was crushed, or so she said, yet she was easily persuaded that the Sherry house was the proper showcase for her new gown. The dress came from a bargain basement, and none of the girls liked the color; but it was new, and they were grateful she finally allowed them to buy it.

The bride gave her sisters a choice of soft yellow or green for their attendants' dresses, and they chose swirling, layered gowns of golden yellow.

On the day of the wedding, Alex rode with Lisa to Len's house but not before he had helped Ethel, Colleen, and, finally, Julie into their limousine. Julie had to keep her head when Alex whispered something for her alone.

"You look absolutely beautiful. How do you expect me not to love you?"

Julie didn't answer. His eyes held hers as they drove away.

Sitting on a mound far back from the road, the magnificent Sherry estate was enclosed by a stone wall and surrounded with historic maples, pines, and oaks. It reminded Julie of an ancient castle, gazing down with disdain on trendy, fashionable Kansas City. The limousines took them through iron gates guarded by security police. At the end of a long drive, uniformed attendants, who were parking cars, helped them from their automobiles.

Settling their dresses, they gave attention to the wedding coordinator's directions. Alex gave Julie a last look and went inside with an attendant to join Len. Julie wondered what the men would talk about in those last few minutes before the wedding. What did they have in common?

Decorators for the wedding had blended baskets of yellow mums with selected fall flowers and greenery. Placed alternately with the flower baskets, tall, golden baroque candelabra filled with creamy candles lined the walls and surrounded the altar set up at the far end of the room. In an alcove midway to the altar, a string ensemble played wedding preludes as those invited signed a guest book, greeted friends, and were seated. *Lisa has chosen well,* thought Julie.

At the appropriate moment, Ethel, conspicuous in her orchid gown, was escorted to a seat in front, across the aisle from Len's mother, who had selected a beige lace gown.

Mrs. Sherry's smile got none from Ethel, Julie noted sadly; but it was time for her entrance, and she made herself concentrate on her own part in the ceremony. Following Colleen, she then turned to watch Lisa.

The bride's tiny waist was accented by a bouffant skirt of yards of ivory satin. Beading and seed pearls embroidered her bodice, and sleeves of the same detail ended in points over her hands. Lisa's red hair, coiffed intricately on top of her head, held a gleaming crown. A cathedral-length veil cascaded from it. Len's gift, a diamond necklace, sparkled delicately against Lisa's creamy skin. She had never looked more beautiful. As he waited with his partner and another friend, a Jackson County judge, Leonard Sherry's eyes expressed Julie's sentiments exactly.

Julie prayed, in case Someone was listening, that this would be a good marriage. Maybe Lisa had done it the right way; she had looked at the facts and decided who could fill the specifics she considered important. Now, if she really tried . . .

Julie took Lisa's bouquet of white roses from her hands, and Alex started the ceremony. His glance met hers as he spoke the words of eternal love; Julie felt he was pronouncing vows for the two of them. The ceremony was pulling her in more than she wanted to be. At the proper moment she laid Len's ring on Alex's Bible with trembling fingers. Lisa put the ring on Len's finger, and suddenly she was no longer Lisa Richmond. She was Mrs. Leonard Sherry.

When Julie gave back Lisa's bouquet, her eyes again met Alex's, and the moment was charged with emotion. Hardly able to breathe, she followed the bridal couple back up the aisle. Would they never reach the end? Something she had never felt before was happening. She had to get away.

At the end of the gallery, Lisa and Len were enveloped by the crowd. The couple was kissing and being kissed; then everybody was kissing everybody. Julie saw Alex in the crowd near her. Then she felt his lips brush hers before he turned away to speak to Ethel.

Julie tried hard to fall asleep that night, but the memory of Alex's kiss kept her from rest.

Chapter 7

A week after Lisa's wedding, Mrs. Larabee telephoned Julie and made an appointment to see her on Friday. She gave no reason for their conference, so Julie feared the worst.

When Colleen came from work, she told her sister about the phone call, but not Ethel. Her mother would declare it another of Julie's *failures,* even though it was Sid's failure as a husband that was at the root of the problem.

"It probably means she's letting me go," said Julie.

As usual, Colleen was encouraging. "And maybe Mrs. Larabee and the board realize how efficient you are at your job. I'll bet it's an apology and they beg you to stay."

"I don't feel your confidence, Colleen. But you can be sure Mrs. Larabee will go through the formal procedure. She's a lady who likes things well organized, with all the loose ends tied up. I'll probably get a parchment certificate of termination with a black border." Julie tipped her head to one side and eyed Colleen up and down. "Are you feeling okay, honey? I think you've lost weight."

"Does it show?" Colleen asked with a smile. "I'm sure trying. I don't eat lunch now — I walk."

"Hey, that's a good idea, for a while anyway." Julie was worried about missed meals, as well as her safety. "Do you walk alone or with someone?"

Colleen's face flushed, and her eyes shone. "Well, yesterday Curt stopped his car to pick me up; instead, he got out and walked with me."

"That sounds promising," Julie said, urging her on with full attention.

"Not very. All he talked about was Lisa. Her marrying so suddenly was hard for Curt. I guess he thought they were closer than Lisa did."

"So? What are you waiting for?" asked Julie. "Now's your chance."

"Why do you think I'm skipping lunch and walking? And while I lose weight, I intend to make some other improvements."

"How about a short cut with a perm? That should be a good start," suggested Julie.

Colleen hugged her. "Oh, I knew you'd help. You're the best sister in the world."

"Don't forget the one in Aruba."

"I can't wait till Lisa comes back. Do you think she'll still be with us once in a while?"

"I think so. We're pretty close, you know." Julie laughed. "After all, you just can't resign from The Three Zanies' Club!"

Julie dressed in a conservative mint green outfit and tied her hair back with a chiffon scarf of the same color. Her cocoa shoes matched the bag she picked up as she left the house for her Friday appointment. If she was being fired, she wanted to go in looking as if she had a better job right around the corner.

Nita rushed to greet her when she arrived at the school and ushered her directly into Mrs. Larabee's office. The room, filled with fine antiques, was a proper backdrop for Pennington's principal, who came from one of Kansas City's pioneer families. Smiling, Mrs. Larabee rose from her desk to extend her hands to Julie.

"My dear Miss Richmond, how happy I am to see you."

The gesture astonished Julie. "I'm happy to see you, too, Mrs. Larabee."

"Please, be seated, and we'll get right to our business." Mrs. Larabee took a manila envelope from the console behind her desk. "Without going into details, the board of trustees and I request that you continue in your position as vice-principal of Pen-

94

nington." She handed the envelope to Julie. "This contains the paperwork for an upgrade in your salary, plus a small bonus in consideration of your patience."

Julie's breath flowed evenly again. Until that moment she hadn't realized the stress she was under.

"Thank you, Mrs. Larabee," she said, holding down her exuberance. "I've missed not being here this summer."

"Yes, Amelia Stewart called the school several times to ask about you. Apparently she was unable to get you at home."

Julie frowned. She remembered only one call from Amelia the evening Alex had foolishly asked her to marry him. Was her mother deliberately keeping Amelia's calls from her when Julie's job was in jeopardy? She was behind on her activities with Amelia and would have to double up now that she was back at work. Promising herself to question her mother later, she concentrated on plans the principal was outlining for the coming year.

The interview ended with an elegant tea served by Nita, and Julie felt at home again. When she left, Nita glanced at Mrs. Larabee's closed door and walked out with Julie.

"It's a good thing you're coming back!"

she whispered. "I shouldn't tell you, but things have gone from bad to worse around here. Her Highness got the total picture of the work you do when she had to pick up on it herself. I wish you knew how many times she asked me to call you, then backed out. We can't get along without you, Julie."

Julie drove away from the school in a state of euphoria. She had her job back! No one knew how happy it made her. *Forget Alex Stewart,* she told herself. Vice-principal at Pennington was the position for her, and substitute teaching, now and then, made a good job even better.

She felt she could spend money again, so she stopped at a college shop to buy Colleen something new for school. Finding a royal blue blouse with a style similar to her own, she added a gold chain and earrings she thought Colleen would like.

Her mother was waiting downstairs when she got home. "I heard you talking to Colleen about your job. Did you get fired?" Ethel asked, her face sour.

"No, Mother. I go back to work Monday."

"Good. Now maybe that Stewart kid will stop calling." Ethel thumped up the stairs until Julie called out.

"Mother, why didn't you tell me when Amelia called?"

"That pest? Chatters like a chipmunk. I got tired of listening and hung up half the time." She laughed.

Trying to contain her anger, Julie raised her voice. "In the future, please, take down the information I need to call back. I bought you a notepad and pen for that explicit purpose." Her voice softened as she willed herself to calm down. "Has anyone else called that you've forgotten to tell me about?"

"Only the preacher. But I knew you didn't want to talk to him, and I told him so." Ethel continued up the stairs. "If you want anything to eat, go fix it."

Julie was trembling. Her mother was getting worse. No one treated her own flesh and blood the way Ethel did. Lisa got out because she could stand it no longer. Colleen would leave soon, and then she would be alone with her mother.

After trying twice to phone Amelia, she left her number on the machine. She checked her watch and decided to drop by the library. Maybe Colleen would go out for a salad with her.

"Miss Richmond! Miss Richmond!" a familiar voice called, and Julie turned to see

Alex and Amelia hurrying up the wide stone steps of the library.

"Hello, darling," Julie answered, dropping down to hug Amelia, not caring that she'd used such an endearing term. "I've missed you."

She glanced at Alex, and he mouthed, *Me, too?* Taking Amelia's hand, she turned away. Alex reached around her to open the door, and they stepped inside.

High-beamed ceilings echoed soft voices, and, hung by twenty-foot chains, lamps with frosted globes and ornate metal fittings lit sections of bookshelves and tables of readers. Julie loved the smells of the old library: aged leather, printers' ink, furniture polish, even a little dust.

A high voice assailed them. "Is that you, Dr. Stewart?" Mrs. Biddle came toward them from a side room. "Well, you and Amelia are here a lot, aren't you?" she said. "I saw you here last week, but I was busy and didn't get a chance to speak to you." Mrs. Biddle ignored Julie.

"Yes, Mrs. Biddle. With the encouragement of Miss Richmond here — you remember Miss Julie Richmond, vice-principal of the Pennington School, where my daughter is a student? She has helped Amelia push up her reading skills dramatically. We're here to check out another stack of books."

"Would you like to hear me read, Mrs. Biddle?" questioned Amelia with enthusiasm. "You can come with me to the children's section and help me pick out a book you'd like to hear. Then we'll read it while Daddy finds his stuff."

As Alex smiled and agreed, Julie could hardly keep from laughing. It was like watching a cartoon on television. Mrs. Biddle was the last person she'd expected to meet. And in the company of Alex? It was hilarious! She saw him fighting to keep his face straight, but how he had carried it off! Not a single ugly word, yet Mrs. Biddle was backing away, trying to escape both father *and* child.

Colleen spied them, and she parked her book cart to join them. Her eyes were shining.

"Hi, everyone! Julie, who's this pretty girl?"

"This is Alex's daughter, Amelia. Amelia, this is my sister Colleen."

"Are you the one Daddy married?" Amelia giggled. "I said it wrong! How do I say it, Daddy?"

He smiled and patted her head. "You're only a little mixed up, honey. I performed the marriage ceremony for Lisa, Colleen and Julie's sister.

"Oh. Do you work here?" Amelia directed to Colleen.

"Yes. Is there something I can help you with?"

"Tell you what," said Alex. "I'll talk to Julie while you two girls look for books. Okay?"

Julie spoke up. "Colleen, I came by to see if we might have lunch together if it's not too late. I have good news."

"Low man on the totem pole goes to lunch last." Colleen grinned. "I'll help Amelia find her books, and then I'll sign out."

Colleen and Amelia scurried away, and Alex turned to Julie.

"Am I mistaken, or has Colleen taken on a new look?"

"She has. Since Lisa's married, she's determined to make Lisa's old standby fall in love with her," Julie answered.

"How do you feel about that?"

"You know how I feel. I'm not interested in marriage, but it seems to be what Colleen wants. The boy's name is Curtis Graham. He's studying medicine at Washington U. and, as you know, Colleen will be at Lindenwood, in St. Charles — close."

"I wish her well." Alex rubbed the back of his neck and took a deep breath. "It's a shame your sisters can't persuade you to give a guy a break." He hurried on. "You wouldn't like to tell *me* your good news, would you?"

"You'll know it sooner or later. Pennington asked me to come back."

"That's good, Julie. I'm glad they woke up before some other school snared you. As a matter of fact, my congregation had a church-wide business session and, in a manner of speaking, gave me a vote of confidence. So it seems I've kept my job, too."

Julie was afraid to say *I'm glad,* so, smiling, she went back to her own situation. "I think I have my reinstatement figured out. Pennington couldn't stand the pressure of dismissing the sister-in-law of Leonard Sherry, who has friends on the board and is given to sharing his money now and then."

"And Julie Richmond just happens to be one of the city's most devoted educators." Alex let go his characteristic chuckle. "Maybe Lisa did me a favor, too. If the pastor insists on holding a single girl in his arms, it's not a sin if she's Leonard Sherry's sister-in-law."

The four gathered at the library exit to

leave, but Alex was reluctant to let Julie go.

"We haven't had lunch. How about letting me take you two with us?"

"Please, Miss Richmond, do come," Amelia pleaded.

"I don't think —"

"I'd love to come, and I know Julie would, too," Colleen declared. "She just wants to be coaxed."

Alex saw the straight look Julie gave Colleen, but she took Amelia's hand, and they crossed the parking lot to Alex's car. Anticipating her move to the backseat, he took her arm. He unlocked the front door, handed her into the passenger seat, then tripped the locks for Amelia and Colleen.

The small restaurant was not far from the library, and Alex wished the trip had been longer. Having Julie beside him was a heady sensation. It was the first time they had been together since the wedding.

When they got out of the car, Julie stopped for a moment. "What happened to the fancy sports car you use for running down pedestrians? I never see you driving it anymore."

"It wasn't my car. Mine went in the shop for its warranty checkup, and a friend loaned me his little toy. Do you want me to trade mine for it?" he asked with mock enthusiasm.

Julie's laugh rang out. Alex clutched at his chest, and he staggered as if in shock. With puzzled faces, Colleen and Amelia turned back, but Julie shook her head and waved them off.

"You had to be there," she said, giggling.

After ordering salads for themselves and a hamburger for Amelia, Alex had a tough time getting Julie and Colleen's attention off his child. For some reason, Amelia was dominating the conversation instead of letting him talk to Julie. Then Julie told Colleen about the blouse and jewelry she'd bought, and Alex saw his chance.

"When do you leave, Colleen? And do you need a ride to the airport?"

"I leave from International next Tuesday, but I guess I'll have plenty of volunteers to take me." Then she added, "Would you and Amelia like to join the family to see me off? Lisa and Len will be back by then, too. If you think you can make it, I leave at six o'clock — evening, not morning."

Amelia begged to go, so Alex was thankful she was along after all. He looked at Julie, who was not taking the invitation well, and addressed her point-blank.

"Is that all right with you, Julie? Amelia

won't mind staying home if you'd rather we didn't come."

The deliberate way he couched the question irritated Julie.

"Of course not," she said in a haughty tone. "The more the merrier."

On Monday, the newlyweds came home, and the family was invited to the Sherrys' for dinner. Ethel made a pretext of not wanting to go, but Julie knew she was dying to see the main core of the house and also what Lisa and Len bought on their trip. The Sherrys were in the living room with his mother when they arrived. In the foyer, Ethel whimpered softly and turned as if to leave. Knowing she felt out of her league, Julie took her arm to support her. Ethel jerked away and walked ahead. A wink from Lisa signaled Julie to ignore it.

"Hello, Mother," Lisa said, bussing Ethel's cheek. "Julie and Colleen, I brought some terrific things for you from Aruba. Uh . . . you, too, Mother." Lisa slipped her hand into the pocket of a striking gold-brocade hostess gown. A maid took away the Richmonds' purses, and, from the hall doorway, the cook caught Lisa's eye. "I see Juanita is ready for us in the dining room, so if everyone is hungry, we'll let Len lead the way."

Len gripped Ethel's arm, propelling her along, and went ahead with the two mothers, Juanita pushing Mrs. Sherry's wheelchair. Falling in behind, Lisa whispered to her sisters, "It takes planning, but how's that for gagging her before she gets off a shot?"

The three walked into the dining room, holding hands, smiling.

At dinner, Julie and the others heard a description of the Sherrys' honeymoon and of the resort, La Cabana, their paradise on the northwest white-sand shore of Aruba.

That Lisa was happy was obvious; in fact, she was ecstatic. The looks she and Len exchanged, holding hands at the slightest opportunity, the whispered words meant just for the two of them — Julie hadn't imagined that Lisa was so in love. Her sister's courage to cut the apron strings was a risk well-taken.

The Sherry environment also suited Lisa. To Julie, she was meant to be the lady of the mansion. She did wonder if two women could live amiably in the same house, especially if one had Lisa's temperament and determination. But she saw the warmth between the elderly Mrs. Sherry and the new one, and Julie's heart took hope. Since

Lisa had not known the love of a gentle mother, there could be a lifetime of affection between the two.

Colleen's departure day arrived whether Julie liked it or not, and, drowning in sentiment, she expedited last-minute details. How she would miss Colleen! She'd be home for weekends, holidays, and vacations; but she wouldn't be there to talk to every day, and her interests would be different. Again, it drummed in her brain: Lisa was gone; Colleen was leaving. Her mother was the only company Julie would have at home.

When she was feeling sorriest for herself, Alex came with Amelia, and Julie again called up the presence of Miss Richmond. The Sherrys arrived, and while Alex and Len chatted and drank iced tea in the kitchen, the girls closed Colleen's luggage and tried for the last time to coax Ethel to go with them to the airport. Bluntly stating she couldn't abide the company Julie kept, she turned away and went to her bedroom. Julie hustled a belligerent Lisa and a disappointed Colleen out of the room.

"Mother is Mother," Julie reminded. "She has her world; we have ours. Listen! Great things are happening for the two of you. Enjoy them!" she said with a kiss for each girl.

She noticed Amelia standing quietly and wondered what she was thinking. For a child whose female parental model was a kind, sensitive housekeeper, Ethel's stubborn display and their attitudes toward her must have been distressing.

Julie bent down to her. "Amelia, darling, I'll explain all this to you another time. Trust me?"

Amelia nodded and gave Julie a comforting pat on the cheek.

Colleen's face brightened when she saw Curt waiting for the same flight she was taking. Lisa introduced her husband, and Julie thought Curt acted with extreme discretion. Alex kept the conversation lively, and Len responded with his own wry sense of humor. Once more Julie admired Alex for his effort, this time to send Colleen away happily.

Even more enlightening, Julie caught Curt eyeing Colleen in her new red suit, draped with a brightly flowered silk scarf from Lisa. Unless she was mistaken, Curt was taking a fresh look at an old friend. If she knew Alex's God better, she thought, she would ask Him to give Colleen a break and let her have Curt. Maybe she'd hint that to Alex. *What? No way!*

The plane took off, and with it went a bit of Julie's heart. Seeing her tears, Amelia pressed close. Julie wasn't asking for sympathy, but when Alex's arm went around her waist, she didn't move away. She needed nothing but her job. Right? Yet each time she vowed to be strong and independent, she invariably leaned on Alex.

Chapter 8

To be sure she wrote home often, Julie bought Colleen a roll of postage stamps and gave her a mild lecture. A letter came as soon as she settled in at St. Charles. Although Colleen described the school in detail, most of her letter was about Curt. He picked up his car at the airport, she said, and drove from St. Louis to Lindenwood. Julie smiled. Letting go of Lisa must have been easier than Curt thought.

By the week following her return to Pennington, Julie had caught up on her records. She finished a long list of tasks she found waiting and did the annual reports due to the board of trustees. The principal simply wasn't up to the extra work.

After battling several hours of names, numbers, and applications for fall enrollments, Julie was tired and restless. Maybe anticipation of time with Amelia was the cause, she thought, checking her watch. Today they would spend the afternoon at the Nelson-Atkins Museum of Art. When Alex brought Amelia, however, he came inside because his child had plans of her own.

"Daddy has a meeting at four, but do you think we could go bowling until then?" Amelia asked.

It wasn't exactly a cultural event, but it was still an opportunity. Julie could analyze Amelia's disposition and reaction to any number of circumstances.

"Bowling is something I've tried a time or two, but I'm not very good at it," she said, eyeing Alex, who stood back, letting Amelia use her wiles without interference.

"You'll do good! And, look, you're dressed for it, isn't she, Daddy?"

Julie glanced at Alex, who gave her an up-and-down look, and she was self-conscious. Still, her chocolate brown skirt was full, and the beige loose-fitting top would be comfortable to bowl in. She took off her dangling earrings, dropped them in her purse, and spread her arms.

"Let's go," she said and took her jacket from a rack near the door.

Alex smiled and touched her back as she let Amelia lead the way. Julie had qualms about what she was getting into, but today she needed company. The grudge Ethel held against her had full rein now that the two lived alone. Julie had to admit: Alex and Amelia were an oasis in an extremely arid land.

★ ★ ★

The clatter of pins falling on thirty-six lanes, loud voices, music, a busy food counter — excitement in the bowling alley included a lot of noise. Nevertheless, Julie looked forward to their contest. Alex had carried bags containing his and Amelia's equipment from the car, so he arranged for an alley and fitted Julie with shoes.

"Hey, Pastor!" A smiling teenage boy ran up to Alex.

"Hi, Keith! Are some of the guys with you?" Alex asked.

"Yeah." He pointed down the row of lanes, and three boys answered Alex's wave. "We just got here. We'll come over later to see how you're doing," he said, obviously challenging Alex.

"Okay. Let's see what *you* can do," Alex countered and clapped Keith on the shoulder. He turned back to Julie. "I'll introduce you to all the boys at once."

It was a ticklish situation, Julie felt. "Are you sure you want them to know you're with me?"

Alex did a double take. "Are you joking? I'm proud to be with you." He lowered his voice. "It's *our* lives, Julie."

Amelia had gone on and was almost ready when Julie sat with her in front of their lane.

Her face red, the little girl stood up. Julie had been so preoccupied with her own thoughts she hadn't noticed Amelia's anger. She'd had the same expression the day she told Julie she wouldn't try out for the school play if she couldn't have the main part. What had upset Amelia?

Julie started changing shoes. "Amelia, will you help me get started and promise not to laugh if I throw all gutter balls?"

Amelia's face changed like quicksilver, and she laughed at Julie.

"You won't do that! I can't teach you much, but Daddy will."

On her first attempt Julie actually hit a few pins, but she knew in minutes she hadn't the bowling skill of Amelia and Alex. Despite Amelia's slow-moving ball, she'd made a strike her first time up.

"Why, that's wonderful, darling!" Julie whispered in her ear as Alex bowled.

"I guess that'll show those old boys I can bowl as good as they can with Daddy," she said, her face gathering darkness.

She's jealous of Alex's friendships, Julie thought. But how could her attitude be reconciled with the work her father did? Julie saw her opinion validated when the boys came over later.

Alex had an excellent relationship with the

teenagers. They surrounded them when she was introduced, but Julie missed Amelia. She saw her sitting apart from them, watching other bowlers, and she remembered. If Amelia couldn't be the star . . .

The boys went back to their game, and it was Julie's time up again. She left a wide split. Alex came up behind her. Taking her arm, he demonstrated.

"You need to follow through, Julie. When you deliver, your fingers should slide out of the holes without jerking the ball. Then, after you release it, let your arm sweep all the way up like this." He raised her arm slowly. "You're aiming for a spot between the one and three pins."

Alex's nearness was suffocating; Julie laughed to dispel the feeling. "I'm happy if I stay on the lane, and you're giving me tips for an expert."

"Try it next time. You'll be surprised."

Julie did as she was told and made a strike, too.

Delighted, Amelia hugged her. "See? I knew you could do it!"

Alex made a move toward her, too, then stepped back. Julie wondered if it was because the boys from his church were there or if he felt she would resent it. Would she?

★ ★ ★

Alex took Julie back to Pennington to get her car, and he apologized for leaving her. He had just enough time to make his meeting. Julie remembered that Mrs. Blake had loaned her car to her sister, so Amelia would wait at the church until Alex finished. Julie stopped him as he went around the car to leave.

"Since taking Amelia home will make you later to your meeting, suppose I take her out to eat and drop her at the house when we're through? Would you like that, Amelia?"

Amelia popped out of the car beside Julie. "Yes! Yes! Could we, Daddy?"

The look Alex rested on Julie's face was so tender she felt uncomfortable.

"If Miss Richmond wants you with her, I can't think of anything nicer — unless I were free to come along." Julie turned her head but not quick enough.

"Miss Richmond! Your face is all pink. Are you okay?" Amelia questioned in a crystal clear voice.

"Yes, p–perfectly," sputtered Julie. "I have to clean up my desk, Amelia. Then we'll go."

A glance at Alex told her not to look back. But she felt his eyes on her all the way up the walk.

114

Occupied with another of Julie's books, the child waited without complaining until Julie finished her work. When she asked what she'd like to eat, Amelia surprised Julie by deferring to her choice. *So, she doesn't always insist on having her own way,* thought Julie. *Especially if she's treated fairly.*

Since there was little regard for well-prepared food in her childhood, Julie believed children should have a balanced diet. She passed up the fast-food restaurants in favor of a cafeteria she thought Amelia would like. She helped the child select her food but postponed dessert until she was sure Amelia ate a nutritious dinner.

A waitress carried Amelia's tray, and, finding a table in a small gazebo with hanging plants around the sides, Julie soon had them settled to eat. The meal was well along when she brought up the reason she had wanted to get Amelia alone.

"May I ask a personal question, honey?"

"Yes." Amelia was all curiosity.

"You didn't like it when the boys from your church showed up this afternoon, did you?"

"No!"

"Why not?"

"They're always butting in! Those boys and all the others get to be first! Daddy plays football or baseball or basketball with them. They even play board games at the house when Daddy could play with me. He'd *rather* play with those old boys!"

Julie hadn't meant to upset the child. She kept her voice calm and began again.

"Amelia, let's think about that. Your daddy has a whole congregation of people to . . . ah . . . help. Boys, especially, need ways to occupy themselves, so they don't get into trouble. You've heard about street gangs, haven't you?"

"Yes, but these are church guys," argued Amelia.

"Have you thought that maybe they would be joining those gangs if your daddy didn't take time to be with them?"

Amelia forked the last of her green beans and silently ate them. She looked at Julie and frowned.

"But, he's *my* daddy. He should be with me part of the time. He always has meetings, meetings, meetings! Sometimes we don't do anything together for weeks and weeks," she explained in exasperation.

Julie caught her hand. "Darling, I see where you're coming from, and I want to help. I'd like to talk to your daddy about this. Would you mind?"

The girl's expression was anxious. "What would you say?"

"I'm not sure. I'll have to think about it for a while. You trust me to do the right thing, don't you?"

"Yes."

"All right. Now, there's something I want *you* to consider." Amelia stopped eating to listen as Julie continued, "I think it would show how grown-up you are if you told your daddy you understand. That he can't spend as much time with you as he'd like, I mean. Do you think you could do that?"

"Well . . . yes. If you say so," came Amelia's reluctant assent.

"Good girl." Julie leaned toward her. "Now, with a clean plate like that, somebody's going to get dessert."

While Amelia enjoyed a banana pudding, Julie reviewed what she'd learned. Alex had a lot of responsibility; that was a given. Yet Amelia was his prime responsibility, and she needed him. She had to make both Stewarts learn to give a little.

Julie dropped Amelia off at her house, had a cup of tea with Mrs. Blake, then, reluctantly, she headed home. There were no lights downstairs, and the house looked lonely. She let herself in and turned on the light. Calling to her mother that she was home, she took the mail from a table by the door and saw a letter from Colleen.

Tucking the stack under her arm, she checked all the door locks before going upstairs. Her mother's light was on, but Julie didn't feel like approaching her yet. She set her shoulder bag on a chair and flopped on the bed. The mail dropped to her side. Lying back, she found she was exhausted, and something else.

For the first time, Julie was lonely. She was still in the job she loved, and school was starting. It was a busy time. Normally she was keyed up and had to make herself wind down. Tonight was different. It was as if everyone in the world, except her, had something to do, and she was bereft of an uplifting thought. Maybe Colleen's letter would pick her up.

Ripping open the envelope, she basked in the warmth of her sister's message. Colleen was happy. She found school exciting and challenging. She'd made friends already, and she'd had compliments on the wardrobe Julie helped her put together. It was a vote of confidence; Ethel had informed Julie her choices for Colleen showed no taste whatever.

Colleen had been out with Curt, and they had a date to go to the Gateway Arch and the Arch Odyssey Theater on Saturday. Julie smiled at the thought of Colleen in St. Louis, on a date with Curt. Her sister bragged that she had lost another three pounds. But what happened, she asked, when her new clothes got too big? Julie made a mental note to reassure her in her next letter. How she would adore buying clothes for a slender Colleen.

Ethel clumped down the hall. "Can't you tell a person you're home? I thought it was a burglar."

"I called out. I guess you didn't hear me."

"You thought you did. There wasn't a sound until you switched on your light and started rustling paper."

"That was a letter from Colleen," Julie said. "She seems happy at school. She's had a date with Curtis Graham."

"Colleen won't get him. She's a slob." Ethel turned toward her room. "Oh, by the way, that preacher called before you got here. Said he wanted to thank you for something. I wrote his number down, but you already know it, so I threw it away."

"Thank you, Mother."

Ethel didn't leave, and Julie knew her mother was waiting for her to explain why

Alex wanted to thank her. It could only lead to an argument, so Julie kept quiet. She looked through the rest of the mail, placed the bills in a holder on her desk, and tossed the remainder in the wastebasket.

Knowing Ethel watched every move, it didn't surprise Julie when her mother criticized her handling of the mail.

"You think you're the big boss around here now, don't you? You're the only one who can take care of things," Ethel carped. "You might even try to get rid of me so you can take complete control."

Julie looked at Ethel in shock. "Mother! How can you say such a thing? What have I done except try to pick up the pieces since Dad's death?"

"You're taking over everything. Now that Lisa and Colleen are both gone, that makes it easier. I'll bet you want this house, too, don't you? Well, let me tell you — you'll never get it. Never!" Ethel was breathing hard, working up intense fury that had Julie close to tears.

"Mother, please don't say things like that." Julie reached for her mother's arm.

Ethel slapped Julie hard and shoved her backwards over a footstool. Julie's head hit the edge of a magazine rack as she fell against the wall. She was dazed for a moment, but she could still hear her mother's accusing voice.

"You were always there, making trouble, causing me to be sick. All your life! Causing trouble!"

Reaching for a chair, Julie got up, shaking. "Please, Mother, calm down. I don't want to take your house away from you. Don't accuse me of —"

"This house was given to me by Mama and Papa. And do you know why? It was the only way they could get Sid Richmond to marry me. Because of you, I had to give up my sweetheart to marry your father. Sid was the one who got me in trouble, and how I've paid for that mistake! But I made you pay, too." Ethel's maniacal laugh burst out. "You and everyone else."

Tears marked Julie's face. A bump had risen on her head, and her leg was bruised, yet the revelation of Ethel's hate hurt worse.

Her mother rambled on, excusing her moment of passion with Sid when Julie was conceived. Once he found out, the man she loved and desperately wanted to marry left town. Her parents gave her the house, on the condition that she marry Sid, and the older couple moved to Florida. Ethel never heard from them again.

Now, Julie understood. Her wounded

heart continued to beat, but she felt nothing. Her mother had never loved her. She had lived only for revenge, and it was driving her out of her mind.

The telephone jingled. Trembling, Julie wiped her eyes and moved to the instrument by her bed. When she lifted the receiver, she could barely answer.

"Julie?"

It was Alex.

"I can't talk right now," murmured Julie.

"Julie, I can't understand you. What's wrong?"

"I can't talk right —"

"Don't mind me," Ethel shrieked. "I know it's the preacher. Well, he's welcome to you! Get out! I don't want you!" She went out, slammed the door, then opened it a fraction and slammed it again.

"Julie," said Alex, "I heard. I'm coming over. Get your jacket and go out to the porch. She must be losing her mind. Don't stay in there with her. Do you hear?"

"Yes, I'll go," she sobbed.

In less than twenty minutes, she was in Alex's arms. *He must have broken speed limits getting here,* Julie thought, but she was so grateful she didn't care. Her world had turned upside down. In his car in front of the house, Julie told him everything.

"You're not staying here, Julie," he said. "I'll take you to my house. No, you won't stand for that — I'll take you to Lisa's. But you can't stay here."

"Alex, I can't leave tonight. I have to be at work tomorrow. My clothes are here. My car. Besides, I can't just leave her. She's my mother. In her state of mind, she might even feel guilty and do herself harm. We both know she's unstable."

She felt Alex's arm relax. "You're right, of course. She's one of the most pitiful creatures I've ever met. But, Julie, you're the one who may be in danger. If you won't leave, will you at least let me go in and talk with her?"

"I guess when I knew you were coming, that's what I wanted. But, by now, she knows we've talked together, and she won't listen to you. I'm afraid she needs psychiatric help, Alex," she said.

"Leave it to me. There's a reliable psychiatrist in my church. I'll talk to him."

"No, not you, Alex. This is my problem. Lisa's and mine. We'll figure out something."

Alex smiled and kissed Julie's nose. "My stubborn little Miss Richmond. It took a crisis to get you back in my arms, but you're still going to handle everything. Let's see how you handle this."

He turned her face up to his and kissed her soundly. Julie remembered the effect of the brush of his lips at the wedding, but that was nothing by comparison. He pulled away, and in the glow of the corner street-light, she saw him smile.

"It never ceases to amaze me that you can look so beautiful when you cry." He kissed her again.

This time Julie pulled away. "I have to go, Alex. There's a lock on my bedroom door. If I have to, I'll use it." Looking back at him, she said softly, "Our relationship has been a rocky one, Alex, but I do appreciate your wanting to help me. I'll call you tomorrow."

"Wait, Julie." He bowed his head. "Dear God, keep Julie safe tonight. She means more to You and to me than she knows. Help her to learn how much."

He spoke the name of Jesus, and a wave of peace swept over Julie that remained with her the rest of the night.

Chapter 9

"Something has to be done. You can't live with her anymore," declared Lisa.

Julie had made straight for the Sherry mansion the minute she got away from school. Now that she was here and had unloaded on Lisa, she felt like a coward. In this lovely living room with its muted rose and green velvets and its graceful dark woods, talk of last night's wild accusations and hysterics seemed far away — another world.

"Only a person who knows Mother well would believe me, Lisa." Propping her elbow on the sofa arm, Julie leaned her cheek on her fist. "Right now, I'm sitting here wondering why I came to you. I should be at home trying to patch things up instead of making you part of this ghastly mess."

Lisa's blue eyes narrowed. "You're just relieved because you talked it out. The problem is still there, and Alex is right — you should stay with me. Len will give us the legal angle, but we must have Mother placed where she can't hurt other people *or* herself." Touching Julie's hand, Lisa frowned. "She's getting worse by the hour, Julie. Don't you realize that? She has a mental problem. Her violence has gone past breaking dishes and throwing things."

"What about Colleen, Lisa? It would break her heart if we had Mother com . . . if we did such a thing. Alex suggested he talk to Mother. We could try that before we consider —"

"Alex will be home with Len in a few minutes."

Julie jumped to her feet. "Why didn't you tell me he was coming? I don't want to see him. Alex has no place in this!"

"Well, look at you," Lisa grinned lazily. "A guy finally got under Julie's skin."

"Lisa!"

"I calls 'em like I sees 'em."

"You've certainly called this one wrong. Yes, I was with Alex last night. But he's the one who insisted on coming over."

"You didn't say no, did you?"

"How could I? I had no one to turn to, at that moment. Besides, I wasn't myself. I was in shock after what Mother said." Julie sat on the edge of a chair away from Lisa. "Why are Alex and Len together?"

"He called Len, wanting to know how to protect you from Mother."

"And you let me go through this whole thing when you already knew about it? Why?"

"You needed to talk, and I thought I might get more information from you than Alex did."

"I'm leaving," Julie exclaimed, gathering up her things. "I don't want to be here when he comes."

"Too late. My lord and master just drove up," said Lisa, peeking through the bay window, "and the preacher is hot on his trail."

Julie's lips trembled. Lisa hurried to her, questioning with her eyes.

"Don't call him that, Lisa. That's what Mother calls him. Only she makes it sound awful, like a curse."

"I'm sorry, hon. I won't do it again. I promise."

They hugged each other, and Lisa kissed Julie's cheek as the men came through the foyer. Neither spoke at first, and Julie felt they knew it was a sensitive moment. Then Lisa rushed to Len and gave him a hug. Alex's eyes locked on Julie, but she didn't move.

"Are you all right?" he asked.

Julie nodded.

"That's a matter of opinion, Alex," Lisa declared as she and Len came toward them.

"Lisa's upset about what you went through last night, Julie," explained Len.

"She's afraid for you." He invited Alex to sit down, and Alex pulled Julie to a couch to sit beside him. "In my opinion," said Len, "she's right. Why don't you move out, Julie? Get an apartment of your own."

"I thought of that, too." Lisa grinned and said, "My independent sister wouldn't be happy living with us, but an apartment's the answer for now. And we'll help, won't we, Len?"

"Of course. In fact, I own an apartment complex close to Pennington. Some of the suites are furnished. You could move in tonight if you like. There's no need to go back to your mother's house at all," he said.

Alex let out a deep breath. "For my part, I can think of nothing I'd rather she'd do than —"

"Wait a minute!" Julie exploded, facing Alex. "Whose life is this anyway? I'll make my own decisions, if you don't mind."

"Simmer down, Julie," Lisa cautioned. "No one's going to make you do anything. But you should have moved out long ago. I know — you wanted to protect Colleen. If Len hadn't rescued me, I might have stayed and wound up just like Mother — mean and vengeful. Let's go by there tonight, Len. We'll let her know Julie won't be back, and you can assess how dangerous she is."

"I'm not a doctor, sweetheart," Len returned. "But, Julie, I can bluff her into thinking twice about the way she treats you. Your mother must understand that her extreme behavior will not be tolerated."

Julie slumped against the back of the couch and closed her eyes. A tear slipped down her cheek, and she felt Alex's hand on hers. She'd lost her temper with him, yet he was still offering support. She wanted to move her hand, but she couldn't. Why was it so comforting to have him there? Simple. It was because she had wrestled with the problem all day long — alone.

She opened her eyes. The other three were looking at her, not pitying, but with sympathy and concern. Finally, Lisa broke the long silence.

"Do it, Julie, for my sake and for Colleen's. If she were here, she'd vote yes. When we go to the house, I'll pack some clothes and personal things for you, and we'll bring them here. You'll spend the night. Then, tomorrow, Len will get his manager to open the apartment for you. Right, Len?"

"Yes, and staying here tonight would be best. Lisa and I will help you get settled over the weekend." He stood up and took Lisa's hand. "Ready to see what we can work out with your mother?"

Lisa sighed as she got up. "I know I said I'd never go back, but I'd rather go myself than give her a chance to hurt Julie again."

Julie had never been so embarrassed. Alex was certainly seeing all their dirty laundry.

Lisa took Len's arm. As they left the room, she called, "We'll be back as soon as possible. Alex, keep Julie company. You'll want to know the results, too."

Julie wanted to throttle Lisa. She was making sure Alex stayed, and Julie wanted him to leave. They were ganging up on her. Without letting her decide what she wanted, the three of them had planned everything. It was infuriating! Her conscience told her Alex had done nothing, but she was mad at him anyway.

With authority, Lisa said, Len convinced Ethel that Julie was not coming back. She had lingered in Julie's bedroom while Lisa packed the suitcases but made no move to stop her. She didn't ask about Julie and showed no remorse for striking her.

Hearing the details, Julie did feel remorse. She thought of the bills her mother had never paid, the checkbook she had never balanced, the monthly check to be banked, and dozens of decisions her mother would face for the first time. Ethel was so childlike and naive. What would happen if Julie weren't there to take care of her? She spoke of her concern before Alex left.

"I thought of those things, Julie," said Len. "I told your mother I would have them taken care of. She seemed glad to hand matters over to me." He straightened his shoulders, took a deep breath, and reasoned with Julie as an older brother. "Julie, your mother is an immature woman. A leader suits her fine. Live your own life now. It's time. Her attitude toward you is indefensible. Lisa says you were the one who took care of her even before your father died. That's a noble act, but misplaced. Long ago, she was the one who let herself be carried away; she didn't have to accept the house or your father. Apparently her handsome Romeo type wouldn't marry her, and she hadn't the courage to face the future with a baby and no husband."

"Give her credit, Len. That would be hard for any woman," Julie replied.

"Yet, today, thousands of single women in the same position do that," Alex countered gently. "They resist the pressure to have abortions, they keep their babies, and they live alone and raise them. It takes courage, but it's being done."

"As you said, that's today," Julie argued. "It was a lonely stand to take in her time."

"Len said it, Julie — Mother's immature. She's dependent on everyone," added Lisa. "Your leaving may be the best thing you could do for her. She may even learn to be a real person instead of a paper doll."

"It could start a change," said Alex as he stood up. "I need to leave. I have basketball practice in the morning with the church team before the boys go to school."

Julie remembered. "Alex, I need to talk with you about Amelia soon. I think I have some answers for you."

"Do you want me to stay now? I can, if you like."

"We're going to our suite right away, Julie," Lisa said.

"No, I need time to collect my thoughts. I'm too on edge right now."

"I'll help you and the Sherrys with the apartment. You can tell me then," he said, with a wave to Lisa and Len.

Frowning, Julie started to protest, but Alex was gone.

"Congratulations!" Lisa remarked. "If you keep that up, you'll send him away for good."

"He tries to run my life! I don't need him! I don't."

"Who are you trying to convince, us or yourself?"

Len spoke in a soft voice, "He was genuinely concerned for you when he called me, Julie. Alex Stewart is respected and well liked. You could do worse."

Julie was taken aback by Len's appraisal. Alex had a good reputation; she knew that. He was known in civic circles in the city and was on a committee or two. But, to her, his lack of time with Amelia gave those activities little merit.

"Len, I'm sure he's a good man. It's just that I'm not in the market for a good man. I love my independence. I don't want my future limited by a man. Can't either of you understand?"

Lisa snuggled up to Len. "I don't see my future like that. Len's given me life. I didn't know what happiness was until we were married."

Len's arm around her shoulders drew her close, and he kissed her as Julie looked on. Admittedly, Lisa was a changed woman; Len's love had changed her. But Lisa wasn't against marriage as Julie was. She didn't realize how rotten most marriages were.

"Suppose we give this a rest until morning," suggested Len. "I'll call home when the apartment manager contacts me, and you can move in. I'm sure there are things about the place you will want done, and we'll take care of them this weekend."

"Thanks, Len. I appreciate the way you've helped me," said Julie.

Lisa delivered a sly look. "Too bad you didn't tell Alex the same thing."

When Julie was in bed, she couldn't get Lisa's last sting out of her mind. Should she have thanked Alex? He had offered to help her move. In her determination to manage her own life, she was forgetting basic rules of courtesy.

But Alex took too much for granted. He staked claims where she hadn't given him permission. Always in the back of her mind was his proposal of marriage. If she didn't keep her distance, he might bring it up again. Why was everyone so eager for her to marry? She was happy; she wished they'd leave her alone.

Last night's feeling of loneliness came back like a judgment. How empty she'd felt! But that was a momentary thing. Normally, her mind and time were so occupied she felt her single lifestyle superior to most women's. They had their husbands. She had her work.

In an unbidden shift of thought, she wondered how she would feel twenty or thirty years from now. Would she still be proud of her independence? She wondered why she was analyzing. Had Alex Stewart's appearance in her life shaken her plan for the future? Every facet of that plan was set in a solitary world of her own choices.

Now, for the first time she questioned if she was right or wrong. The main obstacle that separated Alex and her was his God. That He came before Julie was clear. Her family had never attended church, not even on Christmas or Easter. Alex's prayer for her was a new experience.

She tried to rationalize the peace that enveloped her when he asked God to take care of her. There was no explanation. It was just there: instant, complete, satisfying. But she couldn't be a minister's wife. She imagined herself in a meeting with a dozen Mrs. Biddles. *No!* That was not the life for her.

What made Alex go into the ministry? He had education, looks, a good personality. Why tie himself down to a job where his behavior was constantly examined, and he was not free to live as he chose? Whatever it was, it had nothing to do with her. She could never accept allegiance to some superior being she couldn't see. There. She'd come full circle. Alex wasn't the man for her. She simply wasn't interested. Julie smiled and spoke out loud.

"Hey, God, if you're really up there, keep Alex Stewart away so I can go on with my life."

Saturday found Julie set up in a light-filled apartment on the eighth floor of Len's complex. When she learned he was practically giving her the apartment, she protested to Lisa.

"Look, I don't expect Len to charge me less than he does other tenants. I can pay my way."

"Have some respect for my position, please. How would it look if my big sister didn't get preferential treatment? Besides, you're free to do your own decorating, and have I got some ideas for you!"

"I'm counting on it. The first thing I want is a selection of plants. This place is so full of light it begs for them." The doorbell buzzed. "Aha! My first caller," said Julie as she padded to the door in her bare feet.

Suddenly conscious of her grubby jeans and blouse, her hair piled on top of her head yet escaping from a clip, and not a speck of lipstick, she opened the door. It was Alex, bearing a bouquet of yellow chrysanthemums in a white ceramic vase. His slow grin widened, and the light in his eyes danced roguishly.

"Tell me, Miss Richmond," he inquired, "is there any circumstance at all under which you would not look totally delicious?"

Julie felt the warmth of her finest blush. She pulled herself together and took the flowers he held out to her.

"Th–thank you. Come in . . . please."

Wearing a green knit shirt, khaki shorts, white socks, and Nike athletic shoes, Alex entered the apartment. He strolled through, looking left and right, until his eyes fell on Lisa, who was washing the cabinet over the kitchen sink. In a state of dishabille similar to Julie's, Lisa giggled impudently.

"Welcome to the real world, Parson. Grab a sponge. You can do the bathroom cabinets. Len had an unexpected appointment, so consider yourself recruited."

"Lisa! He's a minister, for goodness sake!" Julie chided.

Alex turned, took the flowers, and placed them on the dinette table. He caught Julie's wrist, and his voice lowered.

"Remember the little talk we had about what ministers do and don't do? It applies to washing cabinets, too."

Julie's face warmed again. "Oh, all right," she said, pointing to a plastic pail of sudsy water. "You wash. I'll rinse."

His eyes never left hers, and when he released her wrist, she still couldn't look away. Lisa finally broke the silence.

"Far be it from me to interfere, but would you two please join the workforce?"

Clean windows and cabinets, houseplants, and Julie's new vacuum had transformed the apartment by the time Len called from his client's office. He was bringing carryout food and would be there shortly, he said.

Julie wanted Amelia to see her apartment and to eat with them, so Alex left to get her. He came back showered, shaved, and changed into gray casual slacks and a striped cotton shirt. Len was not there yet. Amelia darted from room to room, clapping her hands with delight. At the dinette window, her look changed to one of disappointment.

"You can't see the school from here. Since you're so high up, I thought you might be able to," she said.

"I think I see enough of that place, don't you?" said Julie.

Amelia nodded, still frowning. "But I thought if you were sick and had to stay home, you'd know I'd be watching from school and praying for you to get well."

Julie bent down to kiss her cheek. "Only you would think of that, darling."

The doorbell buzzed, and Alex answered. Len stumbled in with a heavy box of food. Noticing his shortness of breath, Alex took the box from him and carried it to the kitchen. Len seemed exhausted, and he sat down with Lisa in the living room. Alex helped Julie unload the food, and she smiled with appreciation. It was a feast of Chinese cuisine.

"Sweet ribs." Julie sighed. "I can't wait."

"Then don't," answered Alex, and he popped one into her mouth.

Julie gnawed off a bite and laid the rib on a paper napkin.

"My, you're messy," said Alex. "You have a spot of sauce right there." Alex aimed a kiss near her mouth.

"Alex! Amelia's in the next room."

"You think that would surprise her, eh?"

"Alex Stewart, have you been talking to her about me?"

"No," he said, taking a bite of Julie's discarded rib. "She starts the conversations without any help at all."

Alex knew Julie saw the sauce that deliberately missed his mouth, but she glared at him and headed for the dinette to set the table.

She wouldn't have to cook for days, Lisa told her, and Julie agreed wryly, wondering how many days she could abide the same diet. Her guests were sipping glasses of iced tea in the cheerful living room of her apartment.

Green plants set off white shuttered windows and a white wicker couch and chairs upholstered in a flower pattern. Alex and Len had attached standards and shelves to one wall, and the colors of Julie's books, plus bright Dali and Picasso prints, underscored the charm of the room.

Amelia, listening to their conversation, climbed onto Julie's lap and fell asleep. Noticing Alex's frown of concern, Julie dismissed it until he rose to feel the child's forehead.

"What is it, Alex? Is she ill?" she asked anxiously.

"No, there's no fever, but I don't like to see her this tired. She's usually more energetic than she was this evening."

"Should we take her to an emergency room, Alex?" asked Len. "They could head off whatever might be wrong."

"No, Len, I'm sure she's okay." He went back to his chair and sighed as he sat down. "I have a thing about Amelia, and it goes back to her mother's trouble."

Julie and Lisa traded glances. It was a rare thing for Alex to mention his marriage, and they were both at attention.

"My wife, Christi, died six years ago with a rare heart disease. Her first symptoms were weakness and fatigue. When Amelia gets tired, I try to keep a lid on her activity. She was up late last night, so I wouldn't let her come earlier. No doubt she would have been fine, but I thought it best to leave her at home."

"Does she have regular checkups?" asked Lisa.

"She gets impatient with the number I have done," he said.

"But, Alex, we went bowling," reminded Julie.

"Doctor's orders. He wants her to have exercise. I'm the one who holds back."

Julie looked at the perfect little face and felt such love that she wondered how Ethel could hate her own daughter so much. She understood Alex's caution; he was a normal father. She looked up at him. As if he had read her mind, Alex's gaze was empathetic.

She thought of her own duty. Her job was to solve the problem of Amelia's bad behavior. Instead, she was getting more involved with Amelia *and* her father. Would she start excusing Amelia's attitude as he had? Len interrupted her musing.

"If you're definite about not taking her to a hospital, I think I'll take my child-bride home," said Len. "She looks tired, too."

Lisa and Len left with Julie's thanks, and Alex saw them to the door. Amelia woke and hugged Julie.

"You let me go to sleep and miss everything."

Walking back to them, Alex smiled at the mini-admonition.

Julie smiled, too. "Not much happened, darling," she said. "Just talk. Do you feel all right?"

"Sure. I'm never sick. The doctor says I'm a 'prime specimen.' Do you know what that means? I don't."

Julie told her it meant best of the best. As she passed Amelia's supine body to Alex, his arms rested on hers, and he didn't let go. Julie was caught in his gaze.

"Why don't you come to church in the morning? Eleven o'clock. I'll . . . we'll be looking for you," he said.

It was an unexpected request, and with

Amelia, too, listening for her answer, Julie was thrown off guard.

"I don't know . . . but thank you for everything, Alex."

Chapter 10

Curiosity had gotten the best of her, yet still wondering why she was there, Julie parked her car and got out. She felt as if everyone in the parking lot and in the vestibule of the church was staring at her. She had dressed conservatively in a brown ensemble, but she was afraid to wear jewelry. What *did* women wear to church? Why hadn't she paid more attention to their Sunday garb? If she were overdressed, she would be noticed and gossiped about again.

Wishing she hadn't come, she followed an usher down the aisle to a spot about the middle of the sanctuary, as he called it, and looked around. It was a pleasant auditorium. Walls and pews were white with dark wood trim, and pew cushions matched the blue carpeting.

Alex and another man appeared and were seated a few seconds before the choir filed in. The congregation was singing when Alex spotted Julie, and his wide smile embarrassed her. She wondered where Mrs. Biddle was sitting and if she'd whisper that Julie was the one that Dr. Stewart had embraced, right in the church.

There were many things Julie didn't know about, but she stood when everyone stood and sat when everyone sat. Prayers were spoken several times, and Julie wondered if the people prayed at home or just at church. She remembered when Alex prayed for her; he talked as he would to a close friend.

Energy sparked from Alex as he approached the podium. Normally he wore sports shirts, sweaters, and jackets with slacks and jeans, but in a dress suit and tie, Alex Stewart's presence was overwhelming. Why hadn't she noticed at the funeral or at Lisa's wedding? Julie inspected a visitor's card until she gained composure.

Alex didn't address any particular section of the audience. His eyes seemed to take in the whole crowd. He talked about Jesus again, and it seemed Jesus had close friends called disciples. They helped Him during His time on earth, and they grieved when He was crucified on a cross. But Jesus had not stayed dead. Alex said He laid down His life for sinners and then took it up again. Jesus was alive!

Julie remembered the exact verses Alex read from the Bible. They were in the book of John, chapter 10, verses 17 and 18. She knew because she wrote the numbers on the visitor's card. No way would she fill out one of those. The ushers who took up the cards would think she was chasing Alex.

She didn't know her way around the Bible, but she'd bet Amelia did. She'd ask to see her Bible sometime when Alex wasn't with them. Maybe she'd buy a Bible of her own. She might even memorize those two verses to surprise Alex. Or would she?

At the end, Alex asked if anyone wanted to commit his heart to Jesus, and Julie was dreadfully uncomfortable. She had an idea Alex was saying it to her especially, but she lowered her eyes; and at last it was over. Julie felt her relief must be visible to the eye.

After the service, Amelia showed up sooner than Julie expected. Mrs. Blake hurried behind, but she couldn't keep up; and in seconds Amelia was hugging Julie's waist. They drew little attention, which surprised Julie.

People were busy collecting families and talking to each other, most of them on the run, and Julie felt at ease again. There seemed to be no special dress code. Some were dressed better than others, but that was not important, apparently, for they intermixed at will.

"Miss Richmond, we have to wait over here," said Amelia, leading Julie to a chair in the vestibule. "Daddy told me not to let you get away, and I won't."

Amelia's brown eyes probed hers as if to ascertain she hadn't gone too far. Julie had nothing else to do, so she waited. She complimented Amelia, who was "gussied up," as Mrs. Blake described her. They were almost late because Amelia put together three outfits before choosing the green jumper and blouse she had on. Mrs. Blake said Amelia wanted to look just right because she was sure Miss Richmond was coming. Julie was glad she hadn't let her down.

The crowd thinned, and Alex, tall, smiling, his eyes on Julie, came toward them from the center entrance. Amelia had informed Julie it was where her father stood to shake hands with people as they filed out.

"God answered our prayers, didn't He, Amelia?" he asked as he swung his daughter up in his arms. "Julie, Mrs. Blake has a wonderful dinner prepared for us. Right, Mrs. B.?"

"But —" started Julie, astonished that they had *prayed* she would come.

"Now, now, we'll hear no buts, Miss Richmond," said Mrs. Blake. "Lunch is in the oven, and I've baked the best raisin and apple pie in the world. Come along now."

Mrs. Blake crooked her finger and walked

briskly toward the double doors that led outside. Amelia was grinning with the same satisfaction as her father. They were too much for her, Julie decided. A lady should acknowledge when she was beaten.

Until today Julie hadn't seen all of Alex's house, and she found it utter pleasure. The furniture was not fragile like hers. It was big and wearable, indicative of a man's taste. The colors were neutral but accented with bold, vivid shades. His pictures were like him — the subject matter understood from first look. Were these things Christi had picked out, or had he thrown away everything at her death and purposely employed his own masculine judgment?

Lunch was as advertised — wonderful. The pie, with a scoop of vanilla ice cream, was beyond description. Julie wondered how Ethel had missed the mark so far, when with a little effort she could have produced meals like this one for her family.

Julie shut her eyes when they prayed before the meal. She had seen people doing it at church. Would they have another prayer when they finished eating, she wondered? No, there was nothing more.

Alex held her chair for her when she sat down, and he came to hand her out of it.

Julie's emotions were playing havoc with her mind. In an atmosphere suffused with contentment, she was truly at peace. In the only family situation she knew, peace was nonexistent. Was it possible to have a marriage in which each day could occur without screams and accusations and threats?

"Penny for your thoughts," Alex murmured as they sat together in the living room.

When Amelia placed herself between them in play clothes that Mrs. Blake had ordered, Julie cuddled the little girl close. Looking over her head at Alex, she answered his query.

"I was thinking how peaceful your home is," Julie confessed. "You're a lucky man." She kissed Amelia's shiny bangs. "And so are you, darling."

"Daddy, don't you love the way she says darling?" asked Amelia, looking up at Alex.

Alex looked deep into Julie's eyes. "I love it, darling." Then he tousled Amelia's hair. "How would you girls like to drive out to see the fall leaves? They're beautiful in the country."

Amelia jumped to her feet, her eyes shining. "You mean you don't have a single meeting this afternoon?"

"Not a one. We have almost five whole

hours together."

"Please, let's go, Miss Richmond. You don't have any meetings this afternoon, do you?"

"No, honey."

Amelia grabbed her hand. "Then come on, before the telephone rings and Daddy has to go somewhere."

Poor little girl, Julie thought. Even when she has time with him, she's never sure it won't be snatched away.

Some distance from town, driving down a lane on property belonging to friends of Alex, they came upon a small lake with a backdrop of maples that were gold and red. Soon the branches would be bare, but now they were breathtaking.

"Have you ever seen anything so beautiful?" Julie asked.

"Yes, it's amazing what God can create to show us His majesty."

"Majesty. That's just the word." She spread her arms wide to encompass the scene before her. "Just look at the majesty of the hills."

As Julie and Alex walked, crunching the fallen leaves underfoot, breathing in the smoky scent of autumn, Amelia chased a toad that hopped ahead of her along the bank. Alex smiled, and Julie decided the time was right to discuss his daughter's problems. She cleared her throat. Was she actually nervous?

"Alex, let's talk about Amelia." He stopped walking instantly, and Julie brushed back a strand of her wind-tossed hair. "I found out the day we bowled that Amelia resents the amount of time you spend with the teenage boys of your church. I realize it's necessary, but is there any way you could direct a bit more of your time to her?"

"Do you think that's the problem?"

"Partly. Amelia is disruptive at school because she wants the attention of the other girls. I haven't had a bad report on her this year, but Miss Clay, her teacher last year, says it comes in spurts. Alex, I suspect when she doesn't get the attention she thinks you should give her, she gets it at school any way she can. Being naughty does get attention from the girls *and* the teacher."

"It sounds right. But how do I know when she feels neglected? Or is a father supposed to grasp it instinctively?"

"I don't think there's a hard-and-fast rule. But maybe you could cut back until you feel, within yourself, that she's had enough time with you."

"Any clues on how to measure that?" he asked with a puzzled frown.

"I should think . . ." Julie's eyes narrowed as she looked across the lake, its surface rippled by the wind. "I'd say, when she sends you off because she has more important things to do and tells you so."

This time, Alex brushed back the tangle of hair from Julie's forehead. "Teacher, you're wonderful," he said with a smile.

Refusing to be distracted, she went on. "One more thing, Alex. Could you give her a private time at night — added to her prayer time, for instance — when she shares what she's reading? It would thrill her if you could trade ideas and let her show you she's becoming her own person."

Throughout, she had his complete attention. "Julie, Julie," he said. "You've really thought this out, haven't you?" Tracing her cheek with his fingers, he spoke again. "We both handle people. We encourage them, help them, correct them when we have to, and we love them. No wonder you suit me like a glove."

Julie backed off. "Let's not get carried away, Alex. We were talking about Amelia. Our personal lives don't enter into this. You helped me when I needed help. I'm merely returning the favor. All that stuff you said in church this morning separates us, and you know it. We live in different worlds."

"Why, Julie? What do you have against God?"

"I've never needed religion. I got where I am without praying about every step I take, and nothing has changed."

"That's because you didn't know what you were missing. Jesus came to fulfill our lives, Julie."

"My life, the part I control, is fulfilled. I have everything I need."

Looking down the bank toward his child, Alex shouted, "Amelia! Come on back now. You're getting too far away." He turned back to Julie. "As long as you don't have Christ in your heart, Julie, you'll never have everything you need."

"I think I've had all of this I want." She started to walk away.

"All right, Julie, I'll stop. But if you ever want to talk about this again, please tell me."

Don't hold your breath, she thought. But in her heart, knowing Alex to be an educated man, she wondered again how he could choose to *serve* an unseen God, who, as far as she could see, had no control over the world at all.

A letter from Colleen announced that

Curt was driving her home for Thanksgiving, and by phone, Julie invited her mother to have dinner at her apartment. Ethel screamed her answer. If Julie wanted to have a Thanksgiving dinner, she could manage by herself. The answer wasn't a surprise, so Julie wasn't crushed.

Oddly, Lisa's response was indefinite. She wasn't feeling well, she said, and she doubted they'd be coming. Julie had never known Lisa to miss a party. Still, marriage had changed things; her sister was not the same girl.

Aware of the circumstances leading to Julie's getting an apartment, Colleen and Curt came to her instead of to the Richmond house. Julie beamed as she opened the door for them.

"Colleen! I've never been so glad to see anyone!" she exploded, grabbing her sister. "Come in! Both of you! I have hot mandarin tea, Curt. Come have a cup before you go back out in the cold."

Curt set Colleen's suitcase inside the door and helped her out of her coat. Julie was astonished at the amount of weight her sister had lost. She was beautiful from her shoes to her highlighted hair. Curt almost never took his eyes from her.

As they talked at the table, Julie got more

clues about the couple's relationship.

"You look marvelous, Colleen," said Julie. "Don't you think so, Curt?"

"Too marvelous. I had to take a number for the privilege of driving her home to KC."

Colleen gave his hand a smack. "Curt, stop exaggerating."

"I'm not, Julie. She's turned into a femme fatale. I have to make her go out with me."

"Not because I am so utterly charming to other men. It's because you need to study, *Doctor*." Colleen turned on a proud look. "Julie, he made the highest grade in the class on his last test."

Noticing the intimate look Curt gave Colleen, Julie felt things were coming her sister's way at last. Despite her happiness with Curt, however, Colleen was concerned about the family crisis.

"Okay, Julie, Curt knows our problems with Mother, so let's get on with it. Where are we having Thanksgiving?"

Julie glanced at Curt. "Will you be with us, Curt? I warn you — it's going to be cozy because I'm having it here."

"Don't apologize, Julie. I think your apartment is gorgeous," said Colleen. "Don't you, Curt?"

"It's great. Only I'm afraid you can't count on me; the folks are looking forward to my eating with the family. We all hoped Colleen would be with us, but as things stand, I guess you want her here. I'd like to come over later though."

Julie nodded. "You know you're welcome anytime you can make it. I appreciate your bringing Colleen home. I've missed her so much, and, with all our troubles, I need a big dose of my sister, right now. Understand?" she asked plaintively.

Nodding, Curt grinned, finished his tea, and picked up his coat. "Good tea, Julie. Thanks." Then, speaking softly to Colleen, "Want to walk me to the door?"

Julie stayed out of sight until he was gone. A shiny-eyed Colleen giggled and hugged Julie when she was back.

"Did you ever see anyone so terrific? And he loves me, Julie. We talk about marriage as if it were some other couple, but we both mean it to happen for us someday."

"What a relief. I was afraid you would quit school and try to support him."

"No, I wouldn't quit. I need these four years to adjust to normal living." Colleen massaged her forehead. "I even dread Mother's coming here to eat. I'm afraid she'll make me lose my confidence all over again."

"We won't let that happen, Colleen, and

she may not come. But don't worry — she isn't going to mess us up this time."

The telephone rang, and Julie answered.

"Hi. It's me," said Alex. "First, Amelia wants to know what time we're to come for dinner on Thursday. Second, Mrs. Blake wants to know if there's any way she can help you."

"Did you invite her, Alex?" Julie saw Colleen's quick glance and smile. "I don't want her troubling herself if she's not eating with us."

"I tried, but she wants to join her sister's family. What about that raisin and apple pie you enjoyed so much?"

"Mmm . . . I can't say no to that." Julie looked at Colleen. "Curt drove my sister home from college. They got in a few minutes ago."

"Tell her hello for me, and I'll see her Thanksgiving Day."

Working with Colleen, Julie thought the holiday dinner turned out well. She anticipated a disaster since she was not an experienced cook, but Colleen gave her confidence; and no tragedies occurred. Ethel refused to eat with them if *the preacher* was coming.

To Julie, it was no contest. She owed Alex

157

too much to renege on his invitation. He and Amelia came early, and Julie was surprised how helpful they both were and what fun it was. Her sister, seizing the opportunity, reminded her it would be nice to have them around all the time.

What Lisa had told Julie was understated. When the Sherrys tried to come for dinner, Lisa not only looked sick, she was sick. She made for Julie's bed as soon as she got inside, and Julie tucked a blanket around her. Once back in the kitchen, she sent Amelia to check on Lisa now and then.

Len said he was no good at cooking, so he sat on a high stool in the corner of the dinette, drank coffee, and gazed out the window. Julie thought he looked like a man with a troubled mind. Had he and Lisa quarreled? Minutes later, she heard Lisa in the bathroom, and Len rushed to her.

When he came back, he helped Lisa into her coat. "I'm taking her home, Julie. I shouldn't have let her come, but she did want to be here. Regardless of how this looks, it's actually a happy time for us." Lisa managed to answer his smile. "We're going to have a baby," he said, the words like syrup on his lips.

Julie and Colleen were ready to swoop down on Lisa, but she warned them away.

"Be careful, I may upchuck on you at any minute," she murmured. "I want to get the elevator ride over and go home. Sorry I'm such a party pooper, Julie."

Assuring her she was not, Julie asked Alex to go down with them to make sure they had no problems. He was gone several minutes and came back with a disconcerted expression.

The turkey Julie had taken up permeated the apartment with its savory aroma, and she handed Alex a carving knife.

Julie examined his somber face. "Wasn't she all right?"

He nodded, then looked toward Colleen and Amelia working in the dinette. "It's not Lisa I'm anxious about, Julie. It's Len."

Chapter 11

Thanksgiving day ended with Curt, Colleen, Julie, Alex, and Amelia playing a board game Amelia had persuaded her father to bring. Julie was anxious for a private conversation with Alex; he had not told her why he was worried about Len. But the others were having a good time, and she hated to interrupt.

The doorbell rang. Lisa and Len were back.

Lisa was smiling. "Yes, it's us! Expectant mommies feel nauseous one minute and not the next, more or less, so we decided to come back for what's left of the party."

"I've married a wild woman," added Len. "She can't stand to miss a good time." He hung up their coats and followed her into the room.

The mood got even lighter, and Julie felt her first dinner party and the evening a complete success. She wished her mother had come. She *might* not have spoiled the day. Who was she kidding? She probably would have.

Pulling his eyes from Len, Alex glanced at Julie as she went to the dinette for the coffee carafe. From the shadows she looked back at her brother-in-law. Alex was right; Len's color was not good. Julie had the feeling Len would be better off at home in bed. She should break up the evening so he could leave. Then, before she could think of a way, Alex handled it for her.

"No more coffee for me, Julie," he said as she started to refill his cup. "I have to get this little girl of mine to bed."

"Oh, Daddy, why? We're having so much fun."

"Because it's past your bedtime, and you need rest. Curt, it's good to see you again, and you, too, beautiful," he directed to Colleen, who glowed at the compliment. "Lisa and Len, I'd say the marriage is going to take."

"You can depend on it, Parson," said Lisa, hugging Len's arm.

"Sweetheart, why don't I walk Alex and Amelia to the elevator?" said Len. "They have the pie carrier, and the food Julie's sending, and the game," said Len.

"Sure. Help them all the way to the car, why don't you?"

Julie kissed Amelia and made sure her coat was buttoned, and the two men, each carrying something, followed Amelia out the door. Curt stood up.

161

"I need to get back to the house, too." To Colleen, he said, "If I ask Julie for some things to carry, will you walk me to the elevator?"

"I shall be delighted to walk you to the elevator, Dr. Graham," she enunciated, "even if you go empty-handed."

After Curt bundled up for the icy chill outside, they left, holding hands and laughing. Lisa leaned back and sighed.

"Aren't they perfect together, Julie? Colleen has made herself over. She looks wonderful."

"Yes," Julie agreed. "Curt told me she's popular with everyone. They see each other as often as he can get away, but his time is so limited Colleen says she feels guilty when he's out with her."

Lisa smiled. "I get the distinct impression that she's his cheerleader, whether it's by telephone, or mail, or in person. Colleen will make an excellent doctor's wife."

"As *you* have made an excellent lawyer's wife."

"The way I was going, I would have been a nonperson if I'd stayed around Mother much longer. Now I just want to love and be loved. But it is nice that I know something of the law. You have no idea how much Len shares with me, Julie."

"Sharing is what marriage is supposed to be about, isn't it? You're lucky your training suits him so well."

Julie was thinking: *That's what Alex said — I suited him like a glove.* Their conversation resembled that of two married women chatting. Only she wasn't married. Then, as if Lisa had read her mind, she said it out loud.

"Julie, as long as you can't or won't get rid of Alex, why don't you marry him?"

"I'm the confirmed old maid, remember?"

"Tell me one good reason you should not try to grab this great-looking man."

With a derisive look, Julie held up her fist. "You want reasons?" She extended three fingers in turn, "Number one, I don't want to get married. Number two, he's a minister. Number three, I could never be a minister's wife."

"You could learn to be a minister's wife."

"Oh, Lisa, that's not something you learn. It has to be part of a commitment inside. Alex wants me to believe in Jesus, and I'd never opened a Bible until I heard him preach. I went out and bought one — don't ask me why. I did it for no reason at all, so stop smiling. I know you and Colleen both think he's the one. But I'm still the

163

same girl, kissed or unkissed."

"So, he kissed you, eh?" Lisa questioned with a sly look.

"Yes, he kissed me. You know when. I told you. I was in shock: After all those years of taking care of her, Mother had just told me to get out."

"That night was a turning point for you, sister dear. Your life has been changing ever since. So don't be dumb and goof it up. Maybe Alex's God led *him* to *you*. That's pretty strong stuff, and I don't think I'd mess around with it if I were you."

Julie was about to undress when the telephone rang. It was Alex.

"I wondered if it was too late to get together again tonight."

"Alex, it's eleven thirty."

"Yes, I know, but I thought you might like to hear about Len."

"Of course I would, Alex. Forgive me."

"I'm downstairs in the lobby. Can we go to the coffee shop where we talked about Lisa's wedding? It's open all night."

"I'll be right down."

Julie ordered decaffeinated coffee, and Alex ordered the same. When it came, he tasted it, made a face, and set the cup aside.

Finally, he started, "Len's sick, Julie. He told me I could tell you, but under no circumstances does he want Lisa to know. She's under a specialist's care, in case she hasn't told you. Her nausea has pushed her almost to the point of dehydration. She probably shouldn't have been there tonight." Seeing her stricken face, he took her hand. "There's nothing you can do; everything that can be done is being done."

"Then what about Len, Alex? How sick is he?"

"It's his heart. The doctors want him to have a bypass, but he's afraid the nervous strain would cause Lisa to lose the baby. He wants to wait until it's born."

"But that's too long. If he's telling you now, you can bet it should have been done ages ago."

"Almost a year. Back then, he turned the doctors down because, even if it cost his life, he wanted as much time with Lisa as he could have. You've no idea how much he loves her."

"Yes, I do. She feels exactly the same. She's told me."

"Now that they're married, he says he can't bear to think of her losing the baby. He's looking ahead. If he doesn't make it, he wants her to have the baby to love and to remember him by."

"Alex," she cried. "Oh, Alex, what are we going to do?"

He slid into the booth beside Julie and put his arm around her. "There's nothing we can do, except pray and do as Len asks."

"What is he asking?" Julie murmured through her choking sorrow and tears.

"Our support. That's why he made an excuse to go downstairs with me. His partner, Dwight Winwood, will take care of his will and property if the worst should happen, but he wants me to take care of Lisa. I told him I'd do whatever he wanted, and he acted more at peace.

"He told me at the wedding he had given his heart to the Lord when he was a boy, and it was still as fresh in his mind as the day it happened. He wants Lisa to start going to my church with him," Alex finished as Julie wiped her eyes.

"I'll come, too. If I go, she'll go." Her eyes met his. "I'll try to learn more about this God of yours, Alex. If He's really there, it looks like we may need Him."

Throughout the holiday season, Julie kept in close touch with Lisa and Len. When Lisa's episodes of nausea permitted, Julie and the Sherrys went to church together.

Len had a good voice, and Lisa and Julie, without planning it, sat on either side of him to listen. One Sunday when they were walking from the church to the car, Lisa chided him gently.

"I love hearing you sing, Len. Why did you never tell me you had this great talent?"

"It's not great, sweetheart. I merely enjoy singing. You know I love music of all kinds."

Since they were eating out together, the Sherrys had picked up Julie that morning. All three shivered at the bitterness of the day. Though the sun shone through a cloudy sky at times, cold wind bit at Julie's cheeks as she spoke.

"This month is full of music at the church, Len. You should have joined one of the vocal groups," she commented and regretted it immediately. Len needed a low-key life.

"I thought about it, but my schedule doesn't allow the rehearsals involved. Besides, Lisa needs me home at night."

"That's right! But I would like to hear at least one program the choir is doing, wouldn't you, Julie?" asked Lisa.

"Yes, and I want to see Amelia's program, too."

"You and the parson's daughter are close, aren't you?"

"If this is the start of a campaign, I'm not getting into the conversation," said Julie.

"That's a guilty conscience talking. You know you should be letting Alex take you out more."

"Call off your wife, Len," Julie said, getting into the back seat as he held her door.

Len put Lisa in and walked to the driver's side. He started the motor and smiled as he backed the car out.

"I'm afraid you won't get much help from me, Julie," he replied. "I think you should go out with Alex more, too."

"Surrounded by conspirators!" Julie shot back. "My own family is trying to sell me out to a man with whom I have nothing in common, spiritually. I'm constantly looking up things in my little Bible to find out what he's talking about."

Lisa giggled over her shoulder. "I notice you qualified what you don't have in common. Don't fight it so hard, Sis. The man's in love with you, and he has a sweet daughter who adores you. How is she getting along in school, by the way?"

"Almost no problems now. Alex says it's because I'm in the picture, and she feels secure. But he'll have to keep her secure himself if I change jobs or move away."

Lisa's eyes widened as she turned to face

Julie. "You aren't thinking of doing that, are you?"

Julie hadn't meant to address this, but she'd set her own trap. "Colleen says there's an administrative position open at her school. It would mean more money, to say nothing of a more appealing résumé," she explained.

"But why, Julie? No, don't tell me. It's to get away from Alex, isn't it?"

"No, not exactly. I —"

"Yes, it is — exactly that!" Lisa laughed and laid her hand on Len's shoulder. "Sweetheart, this is a momentous occasion. Julie Richmond has finally met her match, and if she doesn't escape at once, she'll have to turn part of her power over to *a man.* It's inconceivable!" she finished, giggling.

Len didn't dare laugh with Lisa. He agreed with his wife, but she was handling it the wrong way. He waited. Julie had no comeback and was sitting still, probably simmering inside. He knew his sister-in-law, and it was true — she liked being in command. Lisa, bless her heart, had just stepped all over her big sister's pride. Hoping Julie would forget all but what he was about to say, Len made a request.

"Julie, I don't know your reasons for wanting to leave Kansas City, and I'm sure you've thought it over from every angle. But I'd like to add one other fact before you decide." He patted Lisa's hand on his shoulder. "You know this wife of mine is priceless to me, and it will be several months before the baby is born. Julie, I'm asking you to give up the idea of leaving until well after that. Lisa will need you, and I need you. Will you do this for me?"

Julie could see Len's eyes in the rearview mirror, and she was sorry she had put him through such an ordeal. Naturally she couldn't leave. She was annoyed that she had shared something she'd only lately begun to contemplate.

Lisa had hit on the truth; the problem was Alex. She had seen him every week, and now she was accepted at church as the pastor's close friend whom he might someday marry. Amelia was starting to believe it, too. Julie was getting in deeper and deeper.

Did she refuse to commit her heart to the Lord and to Alex because she rejected a submissive role in life? Alex made no excuses when his messages declared a man was the spiritual leader of the home. If he was the spiritual leader, wouldn't that mean giving up all decision making? Wouldn't he hold the purse strings and insist she quit her beloved profession to participate in things he needed a wife for?

No! It was too uneven. The first thing she knew, she would be walking three paces behind and waiting at the door with his slippers. Julie shook her head as tears stung her eyes. It was absurd to think about. She'd wait until the baby was born and, in a reasonable time, start sending out her résumé.

"Yes, Len," she said firmly. "I'll stay as long as you need me."

"I hope you still feel that way after we eat," he said, looking straight ahead. "I've asked Alex to join us for lunch."

Len drove to a seafood restaurant that was one of Julie's favorites. Not long after they were seated, Alex came. He had turned up his overcoat collar against the cold air, and the wind had mussed his hair. But he was the same handsome, in-charge person with whom Julie feared she was falling in love.

"Sorry I couldn't get here sooner," he said breathlessly, the cold emanating from his body as he sat down. "Lots of things going on at church. I'll have to get right back, I'm afraid."

Julie shrugged and gave the Sherrys a *see what I mean* look and picked up her menu.

"Oh, that's too bad, Alex," said Lisa with

a pathetic whine. "We were hoping you could drop Julie off. Len needs to make a short visit to a client of his I've never met."

Alex bit. With a wide smile, he turned to Julie. "I always have time for that; consider it done."

As they chose from the menu, Julie could not catch Lisa's eye. How could her sister do this, she wondered. It was getting harder and harder to remain aloof when she and Alex were alone, and Lisa knew it. She was manipulating people, again. Worse yet, she was teaching Len. He was the one who invited Alex to lunch.

They parted at the restaurant, leaving the Sherrys to "visit" a mythical client, Julie was sure. Alex turned on the heater in his car, and it sent out a blast of cold air. Smiling, he glanced at her.

"I don't suppose you could scoot over and share your warmth with me until the heater comes on?"

"I could, but it's against my principles."

"Ugh! Those principles of my little assistant principal again!"

She smiled at the word *little* and remembered how small she'd felt when he towered above her the day they met. Her hands trembled as she tucked her Bible into the side pocket of her shoulder bag. Alex was watching.

"Julie, is that the Bible you study?" he asked with a frown.

"Are you checking up on how much I read the Bible?"

"No," he said, "I wondered if you had a better one at home, but you carry this small one when you go out."

"No, Doctor, this is all. I have been reading it; although, I didn't think a Bible had to be a certain size or variety," she finished briskly.

He laid his hand over hers. "Julie, I wasn't criticizing; I was simply interested."

Minutes later they left the freeway and would soon turn onto Julie's street.

"There's something I'm interested in too, Alex. In the time we have left, why don't you explain why God made the man the spiritual leader of the home?"

"What brought that up?" he asked, chuckling.

"You did, several times in your sermons. You really believe that, don't you?"

"Yes, I do." His tone changed. "It's the father's responsibility to make sure his family is taught God's Word. Great women played important roles in the Bible, but it's the man God entrusted with

173

his family's spiritual growth."

"Does that mean he's supposed to think for the wife, too?"

"No, God's Word teaches both men *and* women how to have a satisfying life. From Proverbs 31:10 to the end of the chapter, God pictures a woman helping her husband and children to be their best for the Lord. In return, she has security, peace, and contentment. But she doesn't sit in a corner doing nothing. God gives her a fountain of energy to be creative.

"Those verses were written centuries ago, but they're as timely as ever. God wants a woman to *honor* her husband, but he is to love *her* as Christ loves the church. Our minds are too small to imagine the extent of that kind of love; it's infinite. On top of that, Jesus liberated women with His love. They were mere property until He gave them freedom and status."

They had reached Julie's apartment complex. Alex drove close to the entrance and came to open her door.

"I can't tell you how much I would like to continue this conversation, but I have a rehearsal with the auditorium choir for the Christmas music. Will you read the passage I told you about? And make notes of any questions you have, Julie; we'll talk about them later."

"Yes, I will," she promised, delivering a straightforward look. "Do you realize that, at last, we've been together without bringing up the subject of romance?"

"Wrong," he said, pulling her to him.

Alex's mouth found hers. He kissed her ardently, and Julie didn't care that they were standing in a parking lot, buffeted by the wind, or that her purse had dropped, unnoticed, to the pavement.

Chapter 12

What to buy Alex was Julie's most perplexing Christmas gift. The price, how intimate, and what he would read into a gift were questions her mind shifted about without answers.

She had already given Amelia her gift. Julie purchased orchestra seats for Amelia and Alex to see *The Nutcracker*, performed by the State Ballet of Missouri. On the night before the performance, Alex managed a third ticket for her next to them.

It was a magical night. Julie bought a dress of midnight blue taffeta with a full skirt and a bodice trimmed with black velvet. A rhinestone pin and long earrings of the same stones glittered as she moved.

Amelia's dress resembled hers slightly. Although her full skirt was of green plaid taffeta, shot with a thread of gold, the bodice was solid black velvet piped in gold. Mrs. Blake had pulled back the sides of Amelia's hair and clasped it with a golden ribbon.

"Amelia, darling, you look good enough to eat!" Julie gushed to keep her mind off Alex when they appeared at the apartment.

Although he stood back to admire the two of them, in a black suit, white shirt, and maroon tie with black geometric figures, Alex was the handsome one.

Julie had to tell him. "You look wonderful, Alex."

"Now, Daddy, tell her she looks wonderful, too. Only call her *darling,* the way she does me," directed Amelia.

Alex's eyes were spellbinding. "You look wonderful, too, Julie darling."

"Now let's go," Amelia ordered, and Julie and Alex, taking the hands she offered, did as they were told.

The review of the ballet in the *Star* gave it high praise. Alex concurred; though he had trouble concentrating as he normally would have. The lovely lady sitting next to him was more breathtaking than any of the sprightly beauties onstage. Amelia insisted he sit next to Julie for a reason. That reason had captivated him since the day they met, but Amelia laid it on the table.

"If she sits between us, we can both enjoy how good she smells," she whispered. "Grownups should sit together anyway, and, besides, I can see the stage a lot better than I could in Miss Richmond's seat."

Amelia winked at Alex with the subtlety

of a child who had only lately learned the trick. He was sure both the man in front of her *and* Julie got the picture. Julie's usual blush and lowered eyes gave him an excuse to lay his arm across the back of her seat with a whispered comment of his own.

"I often wonder how men without clever daughters manage their social lives. I know I could never do it."

His remark brought a smile to Julie's lips, and he was fascinated, then thoughtful. *Lord Jesus,* he prayed silently, *You must mean to give Julie to me. I couldn't feel this strongly about her if it weren't Your will. Give me patience to wait until she sees You clearly and gives her life to You.*

On their way home from the ballet, Amelia didn't stop talking, so Julie, intensely aware of Alex, was relieved to answer yes or no at the appropriate times. Having Alex's arm across the back of her seat during the ballet was fatal to an unruffled composure. They stopped at an IHOP restaurant for hot chocolate to top off Amelia's evening.

"Miss Richmond," Amelia said as Julie wiped chocolate from the child's upper lip, "tell the truth now. Wasn't tonight the very best time you ever had in your whole life?"

Julie saw Alex waiting for her answer. Looking at Amelia, she said, "Yes, darling, it really was the very best time I've ever had."

"In your whole life?"

She glanced at Alex, whose eyes shone with merriment.

"Yes."

"I knew it! I told you, didn't I, Daddy?" She smiled at Julie. "I knew that's what you would say, and Daddy said we shouldn't get our hopes too high. But *I* knew."

"You'll have to convince your dad to have more faith, won't you?"

"That's exactly what I said. Also, he has to learn to pray about things more. That's what I did. And see? It happened!"

Julie's face warmed again because she knew this wasn't the last word. Alex's slow grin was there.

"That's right, Amelia. I guess if I want something a lot, I'll have to pray hard until I get it."

"Not only that, but if you want *someone* a lot, you have to pray hard to get *her*," she said with subtlety equal to her wink.

Seeing Alex's embarrassment, Julie could hardly keep from giggling. Thanks to Amelia, he was getting back some of his own.

"I think you've carried this about as far as it needs to go," said Alex. "If you've finished your hot chocolate, we'd better get you home to bed."

The next day, Julie drove to her mother's to take a Christmas gift. The house looked more forlorn than usual. It was cold, and it was December; but none of the neighbors' houses had the dismal look of the Richmonds'.

As she walked across the porch, she noticed one end of the swing had fallen to the floor. Maybe her mother would allow her to send someone to fix it. Strange, Colleen hadn't mentioned it. Did that mean she hadn't been by? No, her sister would need encouragement even to drive down the street.

Her mother didn't answer the bell. Shifting from one foot to the other, Julie felt like a fool. The door had a new lock, and her key was of no use. She couldn't gain entrance to her mother's home. Mrs. Paine, next door, came out to speak to her.

"Keep ringing, Julie. She's there. She's up to her silly tricks again. Are you girls aware of how her mind is slipping?"

Julie nodded in embarrassment and kept ringing. Mrs. Paine went inside, and finally, the door opened a crack.

"Can't you take a hint?" her mother grumbled.

"I'd like to come in and talk to you."

Ethel hesitated a moment, then swung back the door and walked toward the kitchen. Julie knew it wasn't going to be easy. Alex had asked to come with her, but she refused, knowing that if he were along, her mother would not talk to her at all.

"Well, spit it out. What's on your mind?" Ethel asked, her eyes darting around the walls and ceiling.

Her mother's hair was uncombed, and her dress, blotched with food stains and grease, had not been laundered recently. How could the woman live like this? *She doesn't know how bad she is,* thought Julie, and her heart felt torn.

"It's almost Christmas, Mother. Aren't you lonesome for any of your family?"

"I don't have a family. They all died. Mama, Papa, Grammy, Grampa, my aunt Josie — they're all dead, all gone. Sid, too."

Evidence of her mother's decline was plain. She was living in the past.

"Mother, don't you remember your children? Lisa and Colleen, and me — Julie?"

"Oh, I remember you, all right," Ethel shouted. "The day I had you ended things for me. You took my life away, the life I could have had."

"All right, forget me. What about Colleen and Lisa? Don't you want to see them? Don't you care about them?" pleaded Julie.

"Yeah, I know Colleen and Lisa. But I'm going to forget about them, too. They don't care about me. People either hate you, or they die. Except Mama and Papa," she murmured with a smile. "They don't hate me. They love me."

"I know that comforts you, Mother. But I came to bring you this present and find out if I can help you in any way."

The present was ignored, so Julie set it on a chair. From beneath it, a cockroach tried a scratchy escape but was not quick enough. Ethel stamped on the pest with a triumphant cry and danced with delight before Julie.

"He thought he'd get away, but they don't get by Ethel. I watch for 'em all day long, and I kill 'em!" She laughed again. "I handle things around here now!"

Julie wanted to cry. The cluttered house was an eyesore. It was obvious her mother made no attempt to keep order. What could she do? What would Ethel allow her to do? She'd have to talk to Lisa and Colleen. One thing was definite — their mother's state of mind must be evaluated.

"How do you live, Mother? Do you shop for food and whatever you need, or do you have it delivered?"

"Whenever I need something, I call old what's-his-name that Lisa married, and he brings it by. Lisa doesn't know it, but he's my errand boy," Ethel cackled. "Can't you see Mister Fancy-Pants running up and down the aisles getting groceries? I leave out two or three things sometimes, so he'll have to make an extra trip." She laughed uproariously.

Julie dropped into a chair. Her legs would not support her. Len had turned over the paperwork involving her mother's affairs to one of his clerks. But having to do extra tasks for Ethel when his own health was in jeopardy? It was unthinkable! She shook with frustration. Lisa and Colleen had to know this at once.

No, she couldn't tell Lisa. Bragging that Len was the best husband in the world, Lisa might let him continue doing Ethel's work. With school and living away from Kansas City, Colleen could do little to change things. Julie's mind scampered along the perimeter of an answer, and she gave in to it. She had to ask Alex for help.

"I'm leaving now, Mother." Ethel had

started upstairs, humming, as if she had forgotten Julie was there. "I'll call you as usual, and I'll be back soon."

Ethel didn't acknowledge her, and Julie left, worried and sad. Walking to her car, she turned again to the old house where she had grown up and saw its wretched look of despair. She'd have to get the swing fixed, or Len might be asked to do it. Tears misted her eyes. She unlocked her car as Alex drove up, and she knew he had been watching from someplace near.

He strode quickly to her side. Knowing her mother was probably watching them, Julie told Alex to drive to a service station two blocks over. They met at the station, and, as before, when Alex put his arms around her, the floodgate of tears opened. They got in her car, and he turned to listen.

"It was awful, Alex. My mother's losing her mind. She goes from the past to the present and back again. We have to do something about her care. I'm so ashamed. She actually bragged about making Len her errand boy. Can you believe she has him shop for her? She even causes him to make extra trips. We have to do something!" Julie was almost hysterical.

"Shh," Alex comforted, "we'll do something. Stop crying now and listen to me."

He wiped her tears with his handkerchief, then put it in her hand. "We'll talk to Len first. But I'm sure he'll advise us to have your mother checked."

"It's all right to say it, Alex," Julie murmured. "I know her mental state has to be evaluated. And I know it's for her own good. You can't imagine the squalor she's living in. Mother has to be watched, and Lisa and Colleen have to accept it."

"I think Lisa will, but it will be hard for Colleen."

Julie started to cry again. "The house needs cleaning and exterminating, Alex. The porch swing has fallen on one side, and if it isn't fixed, Mother will ask Len to do it. He might have an attack just lifting it." Julie looked at him in alarm. "But, Alex, I'm not hinting that you should do it. If you did, I'm afraid she might come at you and —"

"We'll get it fixed, and the rest, too. I'll call Len when I get home. Maybe we can meet him at their place later."

"Colleen's out shopping with Curt. I'll go back to the apartment and wait for her. Call me when you get in touch with Len, Alex."

Alex started to get out, then reached back to touch Julie's cheek.

"It's going to be all right, Julie. God's already taking care of this."

Alex called before Colleen came, carrying a shopping bag full of gifts. She looked so happy, Julie hated bringing up their mother's problems, but she had to move quickly to spare Len. She'd have to watch what she said; Colleen didn't know about Len's heart trouble either.

After Julie told Colleen they were going to Lisa's that night, she followed her sister into the bedroom, gave her shoes a kick, and climbed onto the queen-size bed to sit cross-legged. Colleen opened a closet door and hung up her sweater and coat.

"Honey," Julie started, "we're going to Lisa's because I went to see Mother this afternoon, and I —"

"Julie! You went by yourself?"

"Yes, but it was all right. She wasn't happy I was there, but she wasn't violent." Julie dropped her head and picked at a fingernail. "She's worse, Colleen. I'm not sure she recognizes reality anymore. And she hates me. You'll understand when I tell you why. But it's her future treatment I'm concerned about, and it's not revenge. You do believe that, don't you?"

"Of course I do, Julie. I lived with Mother

for eighteen years, remember."

"Alex knew I was going there today. He followed and parked where he could see the house. I needed someone, Colleen, as it turned out." Still clutching Alex's handkerchief, she stroked the corner monogram with her thumbs. "He talked to Len, and, tonight we're getting together to decide exactly what to do about Mother."

Colleen closed the closet door. The look on her face hurt Julie, but, as Alex said, Colleen was a mature girl. She would realize the urgency of the situation.

Her sister's answer was a total surprise. "I could have spared you this, Julie, and I'm sorry I didn't. I've shared your letters with Curt, and he prepared me for what might happen."

"Curt! Oh, Colleen, I hadn't thought of that. Thank You, God!" Realizing what she'd said, Julie was stunned, but Colleen only smiled.

"I think that minister of yours is affecting you more than you want to admit."

Julie couldn't argue. What she'd said was spontaneous. Was reading her Bible the reason? She hoped Colleen wouldn't tell Alex. He'd start preaching salvation, as they called it, to her. She sure wasn't ready for that.

★ ★ ★

Colleen wanted Curt to come to Lisa's with them, and Julie thought it was a good idea. A lawyer, a minister, and a medical student should help them make a clear decision. Making the decision didn't take long. Len had gone ahead of them and talked to Ethel's neighbors. He had a lot to share.

Their mother had committed one indiscretion after the other and was a constant worry on the block. She'd paraded outside in her slip when the weather was freezing, and she took newspapers from neighborhood yards every day. She started fires to burn leaves or trash and left them unattended.

Once, the fire department was called, and she was warned. That night, she called the property owner next to her. Julie had started the fire, she said. It was just like that crazy girl. If she couldn't have the house, Ethel declared, she'd burn it down.

Julie burst into tears, and Alex, aware of the others, hesitated only a moment before pulling her into his arms. The room was silent until she composed herself. Len cleared his throat.

"You're not the only one to take a hit, Julie. It seems she tells everyone I steal her money." The girls protested noisily, but Len raised a restraining hand. "Fortunately, I think my reputation can absorb the alleged crime."

Lisa was furious. "Julie and Colleen, as far as I'm concerned, that ends it. When she tries to get at my husband, I'll do whatever it takes to stop her."

Julie glanced at Alex and wondered what Lisa would say if she knew how her mother had used Len. *She must never know,* thought Julie. *She couldn't live with it if anything should happen to her husband.*

Len spoke again, "I'll need the complete agreement of all three of you if we act on this legally —"

"And medically, Len," said Curt.

"Right. So I must hear a vote from each of you."

Julie thought of the votes the three had taken all their lives. It was a childhood thing, then as they grew up they continued it in fun. This time was dead serious. She doubted they'd ever cast votes again.

"You already have my yes vote, Len," said Lisa tearfully.

Colleen, sobbing, turned her face toward Curt's shoulder. As Alex had done with Julie, Curt stroked her hair and let her cry. Lifting eyes to Len's, she gave him a nod.

"I want to hear you say it, honey," prompted Len.

"Yes," Colleen said firmly.

There was no question in Julie's mind what must be done, but when the bitter word had to be uttered, she couldn't choke it out. She knew why; she wanted her mother to love her. Now, she would never win her affection. Looking at Alex, she saw he had bowed his head and was praying for her. Her mind cleared, and her courage returned.

"Yes, Len, do what's necessary to give her the right kind of care."

Len nodded and took his wife's hand. "Lisa and I intend to have her house re-done in order to sell it." He addressed Julie and Colleen, "Since you two have such bitter memories of the place, I'm assuming neither of you wants to live there."

The girls shook their heads.

"Then the sale of the house should keep your mother in a good health care center for some time; especially if the money from it is wisely invested. Property in that area has risen in value over the years, and it should bring a good price.

"Now, be assured that every option will have the approval of you three beforehand. I don't want you feeling your mother was right about my stealing from her. Mrs. Richmond has gone down so fast since your father's death, I doubt if she will remember the house a year from now."

Julie saw Curt unconsciously nod.

"Have you any other questions?" No one spoke. "I'm sure you will have some later, but you're in a bit of shock at the present." Still holding Lisa's hand, Len looked at the three girls. "You'll regret doing this at Christmas, but some things have to be taken care of before they turn into a tragedy."

"You're right, Len," said Alex, "and I'd like to add one more thing. The Bible says we're responsible to give our parents good care. I hope you won't allow guilt to mislead you. Even though it's difficult, putting your mother in a care center is the kindest thing you can do for her in her condition. Be assured that what Len and I arrange, with Curt's help, will be good care. Now, would any of you mind if I asked the Lord to be with us in this?"

Len gave Alex the go-ahead, and Julie was grateful. This time Alex asked God to lead Len in preparation of the legalities of Ethel's case and to give him strength and wisdom from day to day. For the three girls, he asked for understanding and courage.

Julie relaxed, feeling new strength to believe in the future. Alex finished the prayer by asking that the Sherrys' baby arrive healthy and strong. He said, "In our Savior's name. Amen," and the prayer was over. Each couple talked quietly together, and Julie had no doubt they had done the right thing.

Later Juanita, the cook, brought in a tray of steaming cups of wassail. Julie sipped the spicy drink, thinking how obstinate she had been about accepting Alex's help. Now she wondered what life would be like without it.

Chapter 13

Anticipating a dismal Christmas, Julie and her sisters signed the necessary documents Len required for Ethel's immediate care. Painters and carpenters were not starting on the Richmond house until after the holidays. By then, Ethel would be settled in her new accommodations. Alex felt the abject pall that lay over the three daughters' holiday, but there was a flickering light in the darkness.

So that each sister could spend Christmas Day as she liked, gift giving was scheduled for Christmas Eve at the Sherrys'. Curt's family had claimed Colleen for Christmas Day, and Julie was expected at Alex's home. He told her Mrs. Blake had pulled out all the stops to give Julie the best Christmas she'd ever had.

He wondered if Julie and her sisters had ever experienced a real *merry* Christmas. Having her with Amelia and him, and a smiling Mrs. B. in the background, sent a warm glow through Alex's heart as he thought of it.

He had spent a lot of time in prayer about his relationship with Julie. Love had taken him by surprise. When Christi died, he had no desire for another woman to share his life. He wanted no one to take her place, and with Amelia to raise, his church, and Mrs. B. to keep his home in order, he was happy.

He smiled as he remembered the exquisite, angry lady he had met by accident and who'd stolen his heart in seconds. At their second meeting at the school, a glib remark burst stupidly from his mouth when what he'd wanted was to tell her he was glad they'd met again and to ask her to go out with him.

Julie was stubborn and chose not to admit something out of the ordinary had happened. Hanging onto her beloved independence, she came to him only when there was nothing else she could do. Each time she made it clear, though he was not convinced, that the barrier of his religion could not be crossed.

He prayed for the day he would present to her the Savior he loved. In an instant, she would see why no other way of life compared. Once she took that step, he knew she would be as eager as he to share her new-found faith with her sisters.

Julie attended a vesper service Alex held

before their Christmas Eve celebration at Lisa's. Since many were out of town, the church was only partially filled, and Julie sat alone, at the back of the big sanctuary. Putting on a facade of tranquility was beyond her when her mother had just been admitted to a health care center.

Despite her mood, the soft music, the candlelight, Alex's message of hope, and the final prayer of praise gave her peace. There was always the chance that her mother would get better; she had to believe that. Meanwhile, there were decisions to be made concerning her future and Alex.

Mrs. Blake and Amelia, seated close to the front, located Julie in the rear of the auditorium.

"There you are!" Amelia grabbed Julie and hugged her. "We were looking and looking for you. I was afraid you hadn't come." Her face registered a mood change. "I guess I let Jesus down. I prayed, but I didn't have enough faith."

Mrs. Blake left them, and Julie, concerned about Amelia's last remark, tucked the child in beside her to wait for Alex.

"Amelia, darling, why do you think you let Jesus down? You prayed, didn't you?"

"Yes, Miss Richmond, but I —"

"Let's start a new rule, today. Except at

school and with your school friends, why don't you call me Julie? It will be your private name for me. You see, if you were to call me that at school, Mrs. Larabee might think you were being disrespectful. You understand, don't you?"

Amelia nodded, then put her hand over her mouth and giggled. "Daddy and I call you Julie at home all the time. Act–ual–ly," she stated, using her current favorite word, "we call you Julie *darling*. You aren't mad, are you?"

Julie's face repeated its warming trick. Amelia's latest information delighted Julie. She liked the idea that their pet name for her was used in the boldly stated, comfortable home. But Amelia hadn't answered her question.

"About letting Jesus down, Amelia, won't He forgive you?"

"Yes, Daddy says when we give our hearts to Jesus, He has already forgiven us. 'Course, we can't go around doing bad things on purpose. But when we do something wrong and we confess that we made a mistake, we're forgiven."

"You said you let Jesus down because you didn't have enough faith. Do you think not having enough faith in Jesus is a bad thing?"

"Oh, that's the worst thing. You *must*

have faith in Jesus."

Her heart tightened, and Julie tried desperately to think of something else, instead of the faith she didn't have.

The Sherry estate glistened with holiday lights and wreaths at the gates, and, as Alex drove farther up the hill, cedar trees covered with lights blazed red and green. Splashes of red satin, greenery, and sparkling silver stars decorated the front of the house, and glowing candles lit the downstairs windows.

Like the candles, Amelia's eyes glowed, too. "Oh, Julie, look," she whispered in awe. "It's so beautiful."

Julie kissed the small hand on her shoulder while Alex viewed them with an approving smile. Julie suspected he imagined them married, with Amelia in the backseat, as now, sharing the panorama with her new mother. The thought didn't offend her.

Red was the color of the outfit Lisa chose for the evening. The sequined pattern of her jumpsuit disguised a bare hint of fullness. Colleen's dress was new; Julie had gifted her with a coatdress of amethyst, trimmed with jeweled buttons of the same color. It was obvious — Curt was awestruck.

Julie's own dress was of black lace with a

sparkling jade lining. At church she had worn a black cape, buttoned at the neck, to hide it. Alex helped her out of the wrap as he spoke to Len and, turning, handed the cape to a maid. When his eyes fell on Julie again, they held such admiration that the price of the extravagant dress no longer bothered her.

Around the Sherrys' silver tree were gifts for everyone. Though the day started with her usual morning sickness, Lisa felt better as time went on, she told Julie, and now her enthusiasm stimulated the evening's celebration. Julie was afraid Lisa would exhaust herself, but her first Christmas in her new home as Len's wife was a miracle. She should enjoy it as she liked.

The dilemma of Alex's gift had finally resolved itself. Alex had lost his favorite pen, and Julie replaced it with a handsome rosewood pen and pencil set. His initials, tiny, engraved in gold, dignified the pair. Thanking her, he kissed her cheek. Julie bought Amelia a gold charm bracelet, to which she added symbols of a book, a teacup, a maple leaf, and, last, a nutcracker figure.

"I thought the play was my present! Thank you, Julie darling."

Alex's eyes enveloped Julie with affection.

A heavy box decorated in Amelia's definitive style came to Julie, and, inside, she found a leather-bound Bible. Julie, sure Alex had made the choice, sent him a smile of gratitude, but he shook his head and pointed to Amelia.

"She had her mind made up, and we shopped until she was satisfied."

Amelia's eyes sparkled. "Do you like it, Julie? It has lots of notes and maps and things."

"Of course I do, honey. Who wouldn't like such a lovely gift? Thank you!" Julie said, enfolding Amelia in her arms.

Len asked to see the Bible, and Amelia carried it over to him and stayed to point out her favorite verses.

A silver box came from Alex's pocket. He gave it to Julie, and her hands trembled as she opened the gift. It was a cameo necklace. The total figure was a dancing lady with a veil encircling her in the air as she moved. Julie had never seen a cameo like it. It was a stationary subject, yet it was as if she could hear the music and see the movement. Her eyes glistened with tears as she looked up.

Alex leaned forward. "It was my mother's, Julie. She died the year after

Christi. The cameo came from the area of the volcano — Vesuvius — in Italy. I had the original chain replaced. It was so worn I was afraid you'd lose it, and, knowing you, I doubt you'd ever forgive yourself." His face softened as he looked at the cameo. "It is nice, isn't it?"

She nodded.

The lump in Julie's throat made it hard to speak. "This piece must be precious to you, Alex. Amelia should have it. You don't want to let it out of the family." Julie was talking to keep from crying; it was eerie how well Alex knew her.

Alex tipped up her chin. "Someday maybe you'll give it to her yourself if you want her to have it."

Julie knew all too well what he meant. His finger traveled along her cheek as he gazed into her eyes. A spell she couldn't resist was being cast. Probably he'd resent that metaphor; he'd told her he dealt with young people drawn into the occult, with their demonic studies of witchcraft. But that had nothing to do with the charisma drawing her to Alex.

"Hey, you two in the corner," called Lisa, smiling impishly as the maids gathered up their discarded Christmas wrappings. "Come join the party! Juanita's made a batch of hot punch, and we're in deep conversation here."

Alex stood up, held out his hand to Julie, and they joined the others. Juanita and Sarah, another kitchen maid, set out a buffet of holiday food, brightly decorated with the season's colors. Soon, with plates piled high, the group gathered to eat off trays around the fireplace, which blazed with pine-scented logs.

Mrs. Sherry also joined the group to eat. Then she was wheeled away to her suite by her personal maid and nurse. Lisa told Julie she hadn't agonized about Ethel as she expected to. Seeing how charming Mrs. Sherry was to Lisa, Julie thought how grateful her sister must be for a home in which the mother was a treasure instead of a trial. Len's attitude to his mother was a loving one, but clearly, Lisa had first place.

After the first round of eating, Curt moved next to Alex. "I want to ask you a question, Alex."

"Fire away." Alex propped an ankle on his other knee, sipped his punch, and gave Curt his full attention.

"Well, it's this." Curt seemed almost bashful. "At school they say man evolved from an animal. My folks object to that theory. How do you prove to a hardhead like me that God separated man from beasts?"

"Okay, for starters, let me ask you a couple of questions. Number one, if God didn't create man different, why have animals never built skyscrapers or made scientific advances? Number two, why are there no animal records such as those man has handed down from generation to generation? Also, man improves on the tools he uses, and he speaks multiple languages. I could go on, but how are those answers for now?"

No one spoke, and Curt laughed. "Hmm, Alex, I guess I'll have to think about that. I'll call you this week, and maybe we can talk over some other things I've wondered about."

"Anytime, Curt. Call my secretary, and she'll set it up."

What Alex said makes sense, Julie thought. If she gave him a chance, could he explain away the barriers that separated them? He must have good reasons for choosing the life he had. If she understood why, would she give her heart to Jesus, too? No. It was too scary. She believed in things she could see and touch.

Alex watched Julie and wondered what

was going on in her mind. Except for Amelia, she was the most cherished person in his life. But she did not believe in God. He knew he wanted to marry her, and, given the opportunity, he knew he could make her understand why he was a minister. He had to make her see that it was more important than his relationship with her or his daughter. But it would be hard for her to accept until she knew Christ personally.

Len had purchased the board game they had played at Julie's, and the evening mellowed as the contest began. Curt and Colleen used strategies no one else had heard of, and Julie accused them of making up their own rules. Alex and the Sherrys chimed in to agree with Julie, and Amelia tumbled on the floor, laughing.

"Six grownups who are s'posed to know better, and they're acting worse than my friends and me!"

Such an insightful opinion from an eight-year-old produced a few seconds of dead silence, then hilarity.

Suddenly, Len's face sobered, his face took on a gray pallor, and he sagged against Lisa. Curt snapped to attention.

"Quick! Everyone, get up! Let him lie down on the couch."

Alex grabbed the game, and Juanita took it

away. Lisa hovered in Curt's way.

Curt spoke gently, "Lisa, you need to let me take his pulse and listen to his heart."

Lisa stood up and watched Curt anxiously.

"Call an ambulance, Alex." Then to Lisa, Curt said, "You can help Len if you remain calm. He needs absolute quiet while we find the trouble. Don't you agree?"

Her eyes full of fear, Lisa nodded. Alex was back in seconds.

"They're on their way, Curt — five minutes."

Curt had moved Len's body to a position that allowed him to breathe properly, and he removed his tie and belt. He kept a constant check on his pulse, and in less than five minutes they heard a siren on the boulevard.

At the hospital, Alex's arm supported Lisa as he and Julie walked her from the emergency room to the waiting room of the Cardiac Care unit. Colleen and Curt had taken Amelia home and would soon be with them.

Restful colors of sand, soft blue, and green decorated the waiting room. Striped and solid-color pillows of the same hues were stacked in a corner rack for those spending the night. Reading material was available, but until a report surfaced on Len's condition, no one was interested. Julie doubted Lisa would leave the hospital even after they'd heard from the doctor.

Colleen and Curt arrived, telling Alex that Mrs. Blake had Amelia on her way to bed when they left. Curt volunteered to call Juanita and brought back welcome information.

Because she had not slept well the night before, Mrs. Sherry had taken a sedative before retiring. The ambulance driver killed the siren at the entrance to the Sherry estate, so she had not awakened. When Lisa realized her mother-in-law was unaware of Len's trouble, Julie saw a wave of relief sweep over her sister's face.

Two hours dragged by, and Lisa felt herself crumbling. Her marriage reviewed itself in her mind. She thought she was doing Len a favor when they were married. Of course, she wanted plenty back for that favor, but with her wedding, the scheming stopped. She had fallen in love with Len more than she dreamed possible. Wise, considerate, patient Len was the ideal husband, the knight in shining armor she had waited for, and, soon she would have his child.

Tears stung her eyes as she remembered the joy on Len's face when she came from the doctor's with the news. What she thought was a stomach ailment turned out to be the happiest event in their lives. Since then, the unity between them was incredible. Len couldn't die! He was part of her! He *must* live to see their baby.

Sitting together, Alex and Julie waited for signals from Lisa that they could be of help.

"Alex, why do you think this happened to Len? Was it God's will?" Lisa questioned desperately.

"I can't claim to know the mind of God, Lisa, but I know God wants to give Len His best. Did you know Len became a Christian when he was a young man?"

"Yes, he told me that before we started going to church. I didn't even know what it meant until he explained it. He's so wonderful, Alex. God wouldn't let such a fine man die, would he?" Lisa exclaimed.

"I can't tell you how many times I've been asked that in these circumstances, Lisa. But remember this, please — death to a Christian is not a punishment. It's the promise of Jesus he has waited for all his life. What happens to Len now is up to the Lord. Why don't we pray for him to get well." Alex bowed his head.

Lisa closed her eyes and listened. Alex asked God for a safe recovery for Len and for a return to the happiness Lisa and Len had together. He thanked God for Len's Christian ethics and for the opportunity of knowing him.

Lisa was glad the two men were friends. Maybe, during the day, they saw each other and talked about their religion. Religion was something she couldn't share with Len because she had never known the experience he described.

He wanted her to have that experience, but the thought of it scared Lisa. She wasn't good like Len. Now, though, as Alex prayed, she did, too. Promising God to try to give her heart to Him, she begged Him to spare Len's life and to let him live for their baby.

Alex asked the Lord to give them strength; then he added, "In Jesus' name" and said *"Amen."* They sat back, Lisa trying with all her heart to remain calm.

Fifteen minutes passed. Finally, a small, motherly nurse from CCU slipped in to talk to them.

Jumping up, Lisa pleaded, "Oh, tell us, please!"

The nurse took Lisa's cold hands. "He's all right, Mrs. Sherry. The doctor would have seen you himself, but he had to rush back to ER for another emergency. He's confident the episode was a warning, but he wants to keep your husband in the hospital overnight.

"Mr. Sherry must take better care of himself, and he *must* get more rest. The doctor will be in touch with you as soon as possible with more details; but your husband is stable, and you may see him. You may even be able to have Christmas at home."

Lisa felt Julie's and Colleen's arms around her as she cried in relief. When she was able, the nurse took her to see Len.

Julie watched Lisa leave. "This was a near thing, wasn't it, Alex?"

But Alex wasn't there. Across the room she saw him kneeling on one knee beside a chair, his head bowed. Stunned, Julie realized he was thanking God for Len's life. *We all heard him beg God to spare Len,* she thought, *yet Alex is the only one who said thank You.* She glanced at Colleen. Her faced showed the same guilt Julie was feeling. They reached out to each other and bowed their heads.

Chapter 14

Early the next morning, Julie and Alex went back to the hospital. Julie had tried to get Lisa to go home with her the night before, but Lisa wouldn't be moved. She asked that another bed be brought into Len's room, yet, as she told Julie, it was impossible to relax and sleep. If she did, she feared Len's God would take him away from her. The bright day generated new assurance, and, to Julie's relief, Lisa looked alive again.

When Len was released, Julie and Alex drove the euphoric Sherrys to their quiet home on the hill. Dwight Winwood was getting into his car when they came up the drive. He waited for Alex's car to reach the front walk.

"Lisa," he chided, opening her door, "can't you take better care of your boss than this?" He clicked his tongue at her as she got out of the car. "How do you expect a man to have a happy Christmas when he's worried about his friends?"

Julie watched Lisa's face light as she spoke. "He's going to be okay, Dwight. The doctor wants him to take it easy for a while because he's been overworking. I intend to give him the best care possible."

Lisa's problem has taken her mind off Mother, Julie thought, as she watched Dwight clap Len on the shoulder and hug him. *If this hadn't happened to faithful Len, we would all be drawing on his strength to get us through the next weeks.* But Len had detailed Ethel's case to his partner, and now it would be Dwight Winwood's directions they would follow.

Once he was satisfied with Lisa's report on her husband, Dwight told Julie and Alex he would talk to all three girls before Colleen went back to Lindenwood. Dwight's serene temperament matched Len's, so Julie was sure he would handle everything to their mother's greatest good.

Over the next four days Len began to feel better, and Julie saw Lisa's confidence return. The long talks he had with Alex helped Len regain vitality, and Julie wondered how Alex did it.

"What do you think they talk about in those sessions in the library?" Julie asked Lisa as they waited for the men to join them in the solarium.

"Religion, I guess. Len tries to share the Bible with me, but I just don't get it, Julie. Why is saying 'I want Jesus to come into my heart' so important?"

Julie's heart beat faster. So Len was saying the same things to Lisa that Alex said to her. Was she as cherished by Alex as Lisa was by Len? Yet both men were willing to risk a rift in their relationships to convince Lisa and Julie that Jesus should be first in their lives. Why *was* it so important to them?

Julie and Alex left Len resting in bed with Lisa curled up in a chair at his side. In the foyer, they met old Mrs. Sherry and her maid coming out of the elevator, dressed to go outside. "It's good to see you again, Mrs. Sherry," said Alex. "Len seems to enjoy being at home."

"Yes," she replied. "I'm glad he's taking some time off. He looked so tired, but Lisa's making him rest. She won't let him do a thing for himself. You're lucky to have such a sweet, caring sister," she told Julie. "She's a lovely daughter."

Julie was barely able to manage a thank-you. Lisa had kept the truth of Len's illness from Mrs. Sherry out of love. How their lives had changed in the past months! Here was Lisa, given a second chance, living in an ideal home, expecting Len's child. Colleen and Curt were already looking forward to marriage, and she and Alex . . . As Alex steered the car down the long drive, Julie studied his profile and thought about the future.

"Just because I'm not looking at you doesn't mean I don't feel your scrutiny. What has you puzzled, Julie darling?"

"I saw you smile when Amelia called me that." Alex grinned, and Julie went on, "Lisa and I were wondering why you and Len have private talks." Alex's face sobered. "I think she feels shut out, and I guess I do, too."

Parking the car beside a tree at the edge of the drive, Alex turned off the motor.

"Mostly it's answers to his questions about God's Word. He wants to learn as much as he can."

"He's afraid he's going to die, isn't he?"

"No, not afraid, Julie. That's already settled for him. He wants to know his Savior better." Alex laid his hand on Julie's shoulder. "Len's concern is mostly for Lisa. He has arranged for Lisa and the baby to be taken care of, monetarily, but more than anything he wants Lisa to commit her heart to Jesus."

"She's having trouble with that. Lisa just told me. She's scared. So am I."

"Could I venture a guess why you are?" asked Alex.

It took a few seconds for Julie to give Alex a nod.

"The Lord is working in your hearts. The two of you, and Colleen, have lived in a maelstrom of discord most of your lives. Yet each of you is coming from a different direction. Lisa's treatment was less harsh, and Len came along for her. Because she was ready for his kind of love, marriage has been a kind of therapy for her. Colleen is young and will have several years close to Curt to unlearn some of the anguish dealt her. In fact, it's already underway.

"You, my love, built a wall around your heart because you were allotted the hardest blows. You did it to protect yourself. Your parents' marriage was an example that was always before you, so their failure became the standard by which you judge marriage. But the bottom line is, not one of you were given the chance to know God. Naturally, the unknown is scary to you.

"Don't turn away, Julie," he said, reaching for her hand. "Your parents' treatment taught you to be tough in a tough world, but they didn't give you the unfailing security you are entitled to — that is, belief in Jesus as your Savior."

"You're right about that, Alex. I don't recall His name ever being mentioned in our house. The way you talk about your God with such reverence has always astonished me, but the night at the hospital, when I saw you kneel and thank Him, I finally understood how much your faith means to you. It's like the air you breathe. You would never give it up."

"I couldn't. To me, there is no other life. Nothing else makes sense. God's reason for creating man was to be real to him in a person-to-person relationship. I want Him to be real to you, as Len wants it for Lisa."

Julie had no reply, but forgetting the fervor with which Alex spoke was impossible.

The telephone was ringing when Julie let herself into her apartment. She ran to catch it and barked a hello.

"Julie," came a sobbing voice, "I need you. Come back."

"Lisa? What is it?"

"The doc–doctor is here. . . . He's dead, Julie."

"Whaat?"

"Come back, Julie, I need you."

"I'll be there as soon as possible."

Julie put down the phone in shock. Her hand would hardly obey her. Lisa must be mistaken. How could Len be dead? They had just left him! She had to get Alex. Her hand shook so she could hardly punch in the numbers. On her fourth attempt, she managed the right digits. Mrs. Blake answered.

"It's Julie, Mrs. Blake. Alex is on his way home. When he gets there, tell him to go back to the Sherrys'. Tell him I think Len is dead. I'm going there now."

Julie hung up, grabbed her purse, keys, and umbrella, and locked the door behind her. It was beginning to rain and she could feel ice in it. She drove carefully. It was no time for an accident.

The slow drive gave her time to think. Deep down, she knew Len was gone. *That's how death is,* Julie thought, her heart thudding. *One minute, everything is right; the next, nothing is.*

Could Lisa manage? She had security; Len had seen to that. But could she stand the shock of Len's death so soon after their father's? And what about the baby? Alex had said the baby would be Lisa's anchor, but what if he was wrong? Lisa was opening her mind, trying to understand why Len was so close to God, and God had taken Len from her. Was that a loving God?

Thoughts tumbled in Julie's mind until she could no longer think of Len's death. Finally, the entrance to the Sherry estate came into view. Julie took a deep breath and braced herself for what lay ahead. The first time she prayed, she had yelled at God, joking as she asked him to keep Alex Stewart away. Now, the one person she wanted to see was Alex, and she prayed that God would send him soon.

A maid let Julie into the house and hurried her to Lisa's sitting room. Lisa came toward her with tear-stained eyes.

"Alex will be here soon, honey. He's on his way," Julie said as she gathered Lisa in her arms.

Lisa couldn't speak, so Julie sat with her, mothering her as she had when they were children. They telephoned no one. Lisa wanted Alex to break the terrible news to Mrs. Sherry, before they called the funeral home.

The world has stopped until Alex gets here, thought Julie. *I've never wanted to depend on anyone; yet Alex was the first one I called, and it's so right.*

When Alex arrived, so did order. First, arrangements were carried out, and Julie made appropriate telephone calls, including one to Colleen and one to Dwight Winwood. Colleen and Curt dropped everything, rushed to the Sherrys', and ended up handling dozens of incoming calls. As Lisa and her sisters had loved Len, Julie realized, so had many others.

She saw Alex active at what he did best: organizing, encouraging, and reassuring. He comforted old Mrs. Sherry with words of innate compassion that gave her peace of mind.

Julie and Colleen walked Lisa through the motions of living. Silent in grief, Lisa clung to Alex when he was with her. Julie wondered how Lisa would have managed without his strength or, indeed, how any of them would have managed. Following the funeral, Julie and Colleen stayed at Lisa's house until Colleen and Curt left for school on the weekend.

The staff had moved Lisa to a second-floor suite near Mrs. Sherry's rooms, where Julie and Lisa were trying to relax after Colleen's heartbreaking farewell. A service of hot tea sat on a table between their chairs. Julie stirred artificial sweetener into her cup as she comforted Lisa.

"Colleen hated to leave, honey, but I think it would have been just as hard for her to go a month from now," she said.

"I wish we could be together all the time. But that's a childish wish. I have to face the future by myself. And when the baby gets here, I'll be responsible for him, too." Tears filled Lisa's eyes. "Len told me I didn't have to be alone. He said Jesus would guide my life if I gave it to Him. I didn't understand then, and I don't understand now," she sobbed.

Lisa's spirits were down, but Julie could pull her out of that. It was Len's statement about Jesus she couldn't explain. She didn't understand either. Mentioning the subject to Alex, even for Lisa's sake, was asking for another lesson in religion.

"I think we should visit Mother," Lisa said abruptly and got to her feet. "Why don't we go out this afternoon?"

"Sure," said Julie in surprise. "I . . . ah . . . don't want you to be disappointed, Lisa. She hasn't improved since you last saw her. In fact, she may be worse. I was there two days ago . . . but, yes, let's go again."

She wasn't sure Lisa was ready to see her mother in the guarded care unit. But it might take her mind off herself.

On their first visit to the facility, the three sisters were pleased. Len, Alex, Curt, and Dwight Winwood had made impromptu visits to the place at separate times, and Julie knew when the men recommended the center they felt Ethel would get the best of care.

Shivering in the cold of the wintry wind, the two girls walked past neatly trimmed cedars surrounding the spacious brick building.

"I'll always be grateful to Len for handling Mother's affairs so wisely," Julie said.

"Don't say any more, Julie, or I'll start crying again," Lisa murmured.

Julie returned a wave from one of the patients at a dining room window. When they reached the entrance, a maintenance man, washing the inside of the glass doors, touched his cap and backed up to let them in. Smiling as they spoke to him, they made their way to their mother's special wing. A charge nurse recognized Julie and left the station to arrange for their visit.

When she returned, Julie and Lisa followed her to a room where a heavyset orderly Julie knew as Bud stood by the door. Inside, Ethel sat ramrod straight on the side of her bed.

"Mother," Julie said as they drew near.

Behind them, the door clicked shut, and Bud's face appeared at the double-glass square in the door. Ethel smoothed the material of her warm fleece robe and lifted a sleepy-eyed gaze to the girls.

"Do you know us, Mother?" Lisa asked.

"You're Lisa," Ethel murmured.

"Julie's here, too."

"Yes. She's Julie." Ethel pointed to her.

"You're looking well, Mother. Is it pleasant for you here?"

"Oh yes. Mama and Papa's house is very pleasant. I've always enjoyed living here. They gave it to Sid and me when we got married." Ethel's voice had a childlike quality.

Seeing Lisa's forlorn expression, Julie changed the subject.

"Is there anything you need, Mother? Anything we can get for you?"

"No, I'm fine."

Lisa examined Ethel's face with a pensive expression. It was a situation Julie had already dealt with. Day by day, Ethel had sorted out and kept only those memories that were important to her. Julie could see Lisa assimilating that fact.

"It's a bitter day outside, Mother. I'm glad you have a cozy home," said Lisa, glancing around the pastel-painted room.

"That's because Papa put in storm windows. Mama says we'll be as snug as a bug in a rug all winter," she replied with a smile.

The rest of the conversation followed the same vein, and twenty minutes later, Julie suggested they leave. She was afraid the emotional stress had consumed Lisa's energy. She had all but collapsed in her chair. So much tragedy was hard on Julie and Colleen, but Lisa was having a baby. Julie wondered guiltily if Lisa's doctor would have allowed this trip had he known.

"We need to leave now, Mother. I'll be back to see you very soon," promised Julie.

Ethel didn't move from the bed and didn't say good-bye.

Having stayed until Lisa changed into comfortable clothes and was resting, Julie left. But Lisa was far from relaxed.

The events of the past weeks were always there, repeating themselves, torturing her, not letting her sleep. She saw Len's face before her no matter where she was or what she did. Sometimes his beautiful singing haunted her, recapturing the bittersweet memory of his presence.

Everyone thought she was getting over his death, but she wasn't. Each day made living more unbearable. Why try? What was there to live for? The baby? Without Len, the coming of the baby held no joy.

She could escape, and she could take the baby with her. Alex would shame her for thinking such a thing. But Alex didn't know the pain she felt. He had once, but he had forgotten; or he wouldn't be in love with Julie. Men shaped up and learned to live again. She couldn't.

Alex and Julie would probably marry someday. But even if they didn't, Julie was strong enough to live her life any way or anywhere she chose. Colleen and Curt might be engaged even now, or they would be by the time Colleen finished school. Her mother was well cared for in the health care center. She had gone into a netherworld of unreality and was perfectly happy.

No one needs me, she thought, *not even Mrs. Sherry. She has all the money she needs to be taken care of, and if I* . . . Then she would have Len's money, too. Not even an elderly woman, crippled by arthritis, needed her.

She remembered the prescriptions for Mrs. Sherry that had been delivered the day before. There was a large bottle of Vicodin. She'd watched Nurse Williams lock the bottles in the medicine chest for security. But Lisa knew where Williams kept the key, and the nurse had taken Mrs. Sherry outside in her wheelchair.

Chapter 15

"I'm sorry we hardly got outside," said Mrs. Sherry, "but it was just too cold today. Maybe it will be warmer tomorrow, and we can go out then." She frowned as she let Williams help her out of her heavy wraps. "I want you to check on Lisa right away. I'm worried about her, Williams. She's having a hard time."

"I know, Mrs. Sherry. It's not easy to pick up and go on, but it can be done. We both know that," said the nurse.

Williams situated Mrs. Sherry's wheelchair in her favorite spot by a front window. From there, she could look out over the dormant grounds to the orderly swiftness of traffic along the boulevard. Her patient felt less isolated when she could see the movement of vehicles and people. Mrs. Sherry had led a productive life, even in the early stages of crippling arthritis. Now Williams worked simply to keep her mind busy.

"Would you like something to read, or would you like me to read to you after I see about Lisa?" asked the nurse.

"Why don't you read from the John Donne collection? I feel like meditating on the quality of life," she replied.

Nurse Williams hung up her coat and started to leave the room. Suddenly, she heard screams and running feet in the hall. It was Peggy, Lisa's maid.

"Madame! She's done something to herself! Ms. Lisa! I brought up her dry cleaning. She acts like she's dead drunk!"

Mrs. Sherry seized the brakes of her wheelchair, turned it, and pushed herself forward. Astonished, Williams grabbed the handles and pushed her the short distance to Lisa's suite. In the bedroom, the girl lay sprawled on the bed. Williams tried unsuccessfully to rouse her. Lisa was unconscious.

"Her pulse is weak, ma'am. Her heart's barely beating!"

"Call an ambulance!" ordered Mrs. Sherry. "She must have taken something!"

Peggy snatched the telephone. Without Williams's help, the elderly woman, breathing hard, pushed her wheelchair to the opposite side of the bed. Lisa moaned.

As she fled from the room, Williams yelled at Peggy, "Try to get her up! Keep her moving! I'll be right back!"

When she rushed back, the maid had pulled Lisa to a sitting position, Lisa protesting with a faint "Noo . . ."

Williams set towels, a basin, and a glass of

mustard-colored liquid on Lisa's bedside table. She wished for some ipecac, but the remedy she'd mixed worked almost as well. As the nurse stepped back, she saw an empty bottle near the skirt of the bed. The empty Vicodin container! But she'd locked it up!

"Quick, Peggy! Help me!" she bellowed. "We have to make her empty her stomach!"

Nearby, Mrs. Sherry watched with an agonized expression. Lisa fought against swallowing the liquid, but Williams forced it into her mouth. It started the process.

"Do it again, Williams! Don't let her leave us."

There was trembling in old Mrs. Sherry's voice that gave Williams new determination. She pressed the glass against Lisa's lips. Lisa fought harder this time. Good! Her senseless state might be losing its stranglehold. But Williams wasn't sure.

A siren wailed up the drive. Peggy had alerted the staff, and in seconds, two men in blue uniforms burst into the room. Williams went weak with relief. Her patient's beloved daughter stood a chance now.

"Good morning, beautiful," Alex whispered.

At her desk, Julie flushed as she smiled

and said, "Good morning," in her Miss Richmond voice.

Nita folded her steno pad and left the room with a grin.

"Alex Stewart, you'll have the whole school talking if you don't stop calling at the exact same time every day."

"If we were married, I wouldn't have to call you so often. Scratch that. I'd probably call you twice as often."

Another call saved her from answering. "Alex, hold on while I catch this other line."

"Gladly."

An anxious outburst erupted on the second line.

"Julie, this is Mrs. Sherry. Lisa tried to kill herself. An ambulance has taken her to St. Luke's, but I knew you'd want to go." Mrs. Sherry's voice trembled. "I love her, Julie. *Please,* keep me informed about my girl. I'll pray for her and wait to hear from you."

Mrs. Sherry hung up, and Julie pushed the button for Alex's line. "Alex, Lisa is in the hospital. She tried to kill herself!"

"Let me pick you up. I'll leave right now."

By the time Julie got loose from school without telling why she was leaving, Alex was there. In his car, Julie clasped her hands to keep them still.

"Alex, I let her down. Why didn't I see how depressed she was?" she cried.

"One of the stages of grief is deep depression. My doctor reminded me, and I intended to talk to her as soon as possible. Instead, I let other things get in the way," he said bleakly. "If you're going to distribute blame, include me."

"But I'm her sister. I was seeing her all the time."

"You aren't perfect, Julie. We tried our best to help her, but we didn't get the job done. Let's trust God. He can still turn this around."

"You probably think if she had been what you call saved, she wouldn't have tried it."

"In some cases, saved people do commit suicide. But, Julie, it's not the one who is actively praying, studying God's Word, and serving Him with his life; it's the one who has wandered away from God or needs medical attention."

Julie nodded, wondering if Alex still prayed for her mother. Hadn't he said he wanted to reach all people? Lisa would need to talk to him before too long. Was it time for her to do the same thing?

Lisa never left Julie's mind. With the help of Dwight Winwood, special consideration

227

was given Lisa because she was Leonard Sherry's widow. Dr. Crandle, Lisa's doctor, told Julie that Lisa cried through the official questioning and her psychiatric evaluation. Julie yearned to hold her, but she didn't know what to say. When she was allowed to see her sister, Julie asked Alex to be with her, so he could carry the conversation.

In the quiet hospital room, filled with flowers from Mrs. Sherry, Dwight Winwood, and Julie, Alex squeezed Lisa's hand.

"Len's name is still protecting you, Lisa. Dwight made sure there were no leaks to the media. You're safe."

"You've been good to me, too, Alex," Lisa whispered between sobs. "I must seem pretty ungrateful."

Alex sat by the bed next to Julie. "No, Lisa, I think you're a little confused and need help. Do you realize how God blessed you by letting you keep Len's child? I'm sure Len wanted to see this baby, but he didn't get the chance. So, I think he died secure in the belief that his child was in the capable hands of the one he loved the most."

Lisa gasped and sobbed, "Do you think Len knows I tried to kill myself and the baby?"

"I don't know, Lisa. But I do know this. To take a life, even your own, is a sin. God's Word says so. They tell us the baby is fine, although you almost took away his right to live. But God still loves you, Lisa. He sent His Son so that sinners like you and me could be forgiven and have new life."

Lisa's eyes were locked on him; she was straining to hear every word. Julie listened silently. She didn't want to listen, but she couldn't help herself. Alex had such command of what he was saying.

"Now, Lisa, pay close attention, please. When you took that Vicodin, what were you thinking?"

As Lisa cried, words tumbled out about the futility of life without Len. By the time she finished, Julie felt she had been with Lisa through every minute. She felt the agony. Why was Alex putting her through this?

Alex sat back in his chair. "So, you feel your life is over and you're completely worthless. Is that right?"

Lisa nodded, her shoulders shaking as she cried.

"Since you have nothing to lose, Lisa, why not turn that worthless life over to Jesus? You couldn't feel any worse. Why not see what the Lord can do for you?"

Lisa looked at Julie, then at Alex. "How do I start?"

Alex took her hand again. "Bow your head, close your eyes, and pray. I'll tell you what to say."

Lisa lowered her head and repeated after Alex, "Dear Jesus, I know I've done wrong things all my life and not just when I tried to kill myself and my baby. I ask You to forgive me. You died on the cross because God sent You to pay for my sins. Come into my heart right now, Lord Jesus, and make a new person of me. I ask in Your name. Amen."

Julie listened, her throat tight. Something inexplicable had happened to Lisa. Her eyes shone with a glow from within herself. She and Alex talked about Len's death, and suddenly Lisa's voice was steady as she spoke of the future with her baby. In a moment's turnaround, Lisa seemed to be a new person.

Julie felt like an outsider.

Evening was hiding the last rays of sun behind buildings taller than the apartment complex. Julie stood alone at a window looking down on cars and pedestrians heading home. No doubt most of the people had husbands, wives, or children waiting in warm houses to welcome them. No ponderous cloud of loneliness hung over them.

Colleen, involved with school and Curt, was almost too busy to write often. Lisa . . . her lifestyle had changed, and she was pulling away from Julie. She spent a lot of time at Alex's church — Lisa's church too, now that she was a member. At home she had no one except the servants and Mrs. Sherry. But Julie had questioned her about Mrs. Sherry the last time they were together and got a surprising answer.

"Does she ever come into the main part of the house?" Julie asked. "Do you ever see her?"

"Of course. Oh, Julie, she's been marvelous to me. The first day I was home, she told me, crying, that I was her real daughter. She remembered the night Len came in after asking me to marry him. He was so happy, and it made her happy, too.

"She said she had waited years for Len to find the girl he wanted." Lisa's tears shone. "She was prepared to love any woman of Len's choice, but when he announced that I was the one, she was overjoyed. Overjoyed, Julie! How could I not love a lady like that?"

So Lisa was not lonely either. She had Mrs. Sherry, a gentle woman who would love Lisa and her child. And Lisa had memories of a love she would never forget as long as she lived.

And what did she have? Her same old job, her same old independence, her same old . . . dull life! Why was life dull all of a sudden, when it had always been so satisfying? She'd seen what happened to Lisa. Faith in God had given her sister new enthusiasm for life.

Faith was what Alex said he would never give up. Alex. After years of saying she didn't need a man, she had to admit it. She was in love with Alex Stewart. And she wanted to believe as Alex and Lisa did.

The phone was an arm's length away. She resisted the temptation to call him. She had to think. Alex said faith in Jesus was an individual thing; she had to make her own choice.

In the living room she picked up the Bible Amelia had given her for Christmas. Curling up in a wicker chair, she turned on a light and read random verses. Romans 3:10 said: "It is written, there is none righteous, no, not one."

Maybe she did sin, but why did Jesus' dying on a cross forgive the things she'd done wrong? Alex said that was where faith came in. In the front of the Bible, Amelia had written a reference to John 3:16, and she turned to that verse.

Her heart tightened. "For God so loved the world, that he gave his only begotten Son, that whosoever believeth in him should not perish, but have everlasting life."

Alex believed that with all his heart. He'd told her God's Holy Spirit became part of him when he gave his heart to Jesus. She didn't understand, but she'd worry about that part later. Giving her heart to Jesus was first. But how did you give up yourself? She was getting nowhere. She had to talk to Alex.

Alex was praying in his study at home. He had eaten dinner with Amelia and had answered, it seemed, a hundred questions about his relationship with Julie.

"Why doesn't Julie darling love Jesus like we do, Daddy?"

Alex hadn't answered at first. When he did, it was a considered response.

"Julie has lived a life far different from yours, Amelia. You've always gone to Sunday school and church because your mother and I wanted you to hear God's Word and learn from it. Julie's parents didn't take their girls to church."

"But she goes now. Do you think she will accept Christ?"

"I hope so, honey. I'm praying she will."

"I am, too. But remember what we said, Daddy. We have to have faith," she warned.

Alex smiled — a child's abiding faith. Julie had watched Lisa turn her life over to Christ, yet it hadn't affected her as he thought it would. With her inquiring mind, she must surely have questions by now, but she hadn't called.

He loved Julie. So did Amelia. It made waiting harder.

He couldn't force Julie to talk about her salvation; she'd warned him off several times. He prayed for that special moment when Julie knew, within herself, she needed Christ.

Alex sighed. He had to hear her voice. The telephone rang as he reached it to call her. Startled, he fumbled with the receiver.

"Hello?"

"It's me, Alex. I'm lonely. Would you come over and talk with me?"

An alarm went off in his mind. Could it be?

Her eyes were wide, searching, when she opened the door. As always, she looked beautiful, and Alex longed to take her in his arms. But if her call meant what he hoped, he wanted her to make it clear without any persuasion from him. They went to the kitchen where she poured two cups of coffee.

"I've been reading my Bible and thinking over things you've said in your sermons," she said as she sat down.

Alex placed their cups on the table and sat opposite her.

"Go on, Julie."

"I don't know what I'm supposed to do. Just saying give your heart to Jesus sounds so elementary. There must be more to it than that."

"Julie, have you ever done anything that you'd rather die than have other people know about?"

"Yes," she finally admitted.

"God already knows, and He knows about all the sins ever committed. He can't stand sin, so He gave us a way to be forgiven. He sent His own Son, Jesus, to earth but in human form so people could identify with Him. Jesus was perfect. He never once sinned. Yet He took our sins on Himself and willingly died for the wrong we have done.

"When we ask Him into our hearts, His forgiveness is so complete it's as if we're newborn babies. We don't know how Christ's sacrifice wipes the slate clean for us. But if we, in faith, believe it, God lets us know with certainty that our new life has begun."

Tears came in a rush. "Oh, Alex," she sobbed with a stricken face, "I've been trying to work it out by myself, and I made it so complicated. I should have come to you long ago. I *want* Jesus in my heart."

Alex stood up, and Julie did, too. He took her hands and bowed his head. She waited for Alex to pray.

"Lord Jesus," he said in a tight voice, "Julie has something she wants to tell You."

Julie never dreamed Alex would expect her to pray. She had never prayed a real prayer in her life. But he was waiting, and she found courage to speak.

"I want to accept You and know You forgive me of the things I've done wrong. Please forgive me, God."

Julie felt the dark cloud lift. It was cold outside, yet she felt warm and happy. She couldn't describe it even to Alex. God's Holy Spirit didn't need explanation. He was there.

"Shouldn't you thank Him, Julie?" Alex asked softly.

"Thank you, God." Tears came again. "Thank You for this wonderful gift. And God, thank You for Alex. I love him so."

Alex's arm stole around her, and he kissed her as they wept together.

Wondering why Mrs. Blake was smiling with tears on her cheeks, Amelia took the phone from her outstretched hand.

"Hello."

"Amelia?"

"Julie darling!"

With a catch in her voice, Julie answered, "I've just learned what Jesus did for me, Amelia, and I've given my heart to Him. Now, it seems . . ." She stopped, and Amelia heard her father's voice urging Julie on. "Now it seems I'm going to be your mother, honey."

"When? When?"

Her father took the phone. "As soon as possible, sweetheart. We'll hang up now, and I'll bring Julie to the house so you can give her a hug."

Amelia felt like jumping up and down.

"Oh, hurry, Daddy, hurry!"

About the Author

FREDA CHRISMAN. Deep in the south of Texas, Freda Chrisman and her husband pursue an active retirement. Two married children and six terrific grandchildren assist in the day-to-day process.

Freda is an active conference teacher and speaker. She is past president of the main chapter of Inspirational Writers Alive! — now with five chapters in Texas. Winning top awards in six writers' contests has been a joy, but helping beginning writers achieve their publishing goals is God's special blessing to this author.

She is a member of HOSTS (Helping One Student To Succeed), a ministry of The Master's Touch Program of her church. Together, the Chrismans serve the Lord with the one hundred member "Mavericks" class, Sunday school members whose mission is the true meaning of *Show, don't just tell*.

Freda is a member of American Christian Fiction Writers; the Faith, Hope, and Love Chapter of Romance Writers of America; and Bay Area Chapter 30, also a chapter of Romance Writers of America. That God chose her to write for Him has fulfilled a childhood dream, and writing inspirational fiction has led to incredible friendships. Freda starts the day with thanks for His grace.

The employees of Thorndike Press hope you have enjoyed this Large Print book. All our Thorndike and Wheeler Large Print titles are designed for easy reading, and all our books are made to last. Other Thorndike Press Large Print books are available at your library, through selected bookstores, or directly from us.

For information about titles, please call:

(800) 223-1244

or visit our Web site at:

www.thomson.com/thorndike
www.thomson.com/wheeler

To share your comments, please write:

Publisher
Thorndike Press
295 Kennedy Memorial Drive
Waterville, ME   04901